The
HOUSE
on
HAWTHORN
ROAD

MEGAN WYNNE is a writer and creative writing teacher. She is passionate about reading, writing and teaching children's fiction. In 2007 she founded a creative writing school in Dublin with the aim of inspiring and building confidence in children. Every year she publishes a collection of students' stories in aid of charity. She lives in North County Dublin with her husband and her dog, Beau. *The House on Hawthorn Road* is her first book.

The HOUSE on HAWTHORN ROAD

MEGAN WYNNE

THE O'BRIEN PRESS
DUBLIN

For Dad and Mum, with all my love and thanks.

This edition first published 2019 by
The O'Brien Press Ltd,
12 Terenure Road East, Rathgar,
Dublin 6, D06 HD27 Ireland.
Tel: +353 1 4923333; Fax: +353 1 4922777
E-mail: books@obrien.ie.
Website: www.obrien.ie

The O'Brien Press is a member of Publishing Ireland
ISBN: 978-1-78849-090-0

1 3 5 7 8 6 4 2

19 21 22 20

Cover illustration by Rachel Corcoran.
Printed and bound by and bound by CPI Group (UK) Ltd, Croydon, CR0 4YY.
The paper in this book is produced using pulp from managed forests.

Published in

CHAPTER ONE

Beth stood on the doorstep of her new home dolefully sniffing the salty air. She didn't want to be in Dublin; she wanted to be at home in London with her best friend, Aisha. But since her grandmother died, the whole family had moved from England across a grey windy sea to Ireland.

It had all come as such a shock. One day her Gran was ill in hospital and the next she was dead. Nobody warned Beth it was going to happen, but afterwards they talked as if they had expected it all along: 'Oh she was very sick,' they murmured, 'only a matter of time.'

'Why didn't anyone tell me?' Beth wanted to yell, but she didn't, because Beth seldom yelled. In fact, Beth didn't say very much at all. And since her grandmother died, she said even less. 'Oh, don't mind her. She's like that with every one,' her mother said to complete strangers while Beth stood to one side wondering what she was supposed to do, babble away about anything at all? It seemed so. Everyone admired her older sister, Jess, who chatted about the weather and traffic as if she were forty-five, and not fifteen.

'Our neighbours are rich,' Jess remarked gazing at a gleaming Mercedes parked in the house opposite.

'We've done well to get it,' Bill Boffin said jangling the house keys.

'You mean you've done well, darling.' Sylvie Boffin kissed him slowly on the mouth. Beth glanced up the street to make sure no one was looking. She could put up with this type of behaviour at home, however when her mother went misty eyed and drooled, 'You're the most handsome man in the whole world!' by the frozen peas in the local supermarket, Beth wanted to curl up and die.

Sylvie Boffin wasn't like other mothers. An actress in London's West End, fifty-nine minutes out of every hour she had her head stuck in a script for a play. The rest of the time she spent shouting down the phone to her agent in London, telling him 'he was absolutely useless,' when a younger actress snaffled a role she'd had her eye on.

Bill Boffin didn't roll his eyes when his wife still languished in her pyjamas at midday, put no food on the table in the evening, and left the washing basket piled so high it toppled over. He lived happily on sandwiches and bananas, and as he worked as a vet – and most of his clothes were splattered in fresh pig dung and cow slop daily – he saw little point in washing them.

Taking the keys from his pocket, Bill unlocked the front door allowing the family inside to explore. When Sylvie Boffin reached the small dark kitchen at the back of the house, she made the announcement, which unbeknownst to any of them, was to change number 3 Hawthorn Road from being a perfectly ordinary house to one that wasn't ordinary at all.

'This back wall is blocking out all the light from our south-facing garden,' she declared. 'We'll bang it down and extend into the garden.' Her eyes swept the room. 'It won't take long.'

Three weeks later they were living in a cloud of grey dust and Jess was cooking their meals upstairs on a two-ringed gas cooker.

'If I have to wash up in this bathroom sink once more I shall scream,' Jess moaned peering in the mirror. 'There's dust in my ears, and I even found some inside my knickers.'

'Those men seem to delight in knocking down walls but become mysteriously engaged when they are supposed to be putting them up again,' Sylvie muttered from behind a novel.

Beth's younger brother, Cormac, didn't seem to notice the chaos. Cormac practised his piano scales all day long. Even when Beth shut her bedroom door and stuffed socks into the crack at the bottom, she could hear him. He used to play football and go cycling like a normal person, but that was before his music teacher, Mr Cunningham, declared he had 'exceptional talent.'

Since then Cormac walked around in a 'genius daze' as his mother liked to call it.

Beth couldn't stand him.

She didn't get on so well with her mother either. The only thing they had in common was visiting the local library.

'We'll miss you around here,' sniffed Mrs Crabtree, their old librarian, when she heard their family was moving away from London.

'I know.' Sylvie Boffin sighed. 'It was wonderful living with my mother, but she's gone now, God rest her, and her beautiful house has gone with her. She never owned it, you see. Some kind soul had leased it to her for her lifetime when my father died. So now we have to up sticks. It's very upsetting but Bill has the opportunity to open his own veterinary practice in Ireland. He's very excited about that. His parents live there too, of course.'

'But what about Cormac?' Mrs Crabtree looked worried. 'How will the move affect him?'

Immediately Sylvie put down the novel she'd been holding. 'His coach thinks summer is the best time to move, less disruptive.'

Mrs Crabtree nodded approvingly. She didn't ask how Beth might find the move, even though she fidgeted right in front of her. No, Mrs Crabtree, like most people, treated Beth much like her mother's handbag – something that hung about near her arm, unworthy of comment or interest.

'Well, I hope it all goes well for you.' The librarian smiled. 'Do send us a postcard from Dublin.'

'Of course I will,' Beth's mother tinkled but of course she didn't, even though Beth reminded her twice.

That had been three months ago and now, in late August, the new extension was ready and the Boffin family could finally settle in. Golden light streamed through windows running along the back of the house onto a polished wooden floor in the new kitchen, which was three times the size of the old one. 'What a perfect place to read,' Sylvie exclaimed flopping onto the long cherry red sofa she had bought specifically for that purpose.

'Upstairs, darling!' Bill called from the landing.

Sylvie rushed up to meet him, and Beth heard them giggling in the newly extended bedroom above the kitchen.

'That's them gone for the afternoon.' Jess opened her latest novel about spirits and half earthlings. Every book she read had a black cover and was about something creepy or ghostly.

'School on Monday,' Beth said with a queer feeling in her stomach.

'Don't remind me,' Jess replied gloomily.

Jess was right. Best not to talk about it. School in Dublin was sure to be the worst thing about moving so far.

CHAPTER TWO

Unfortunately Beth's gloomy prediction about school was correct. On everyone's first day, Sylvie stood in the hall fussing over Cormac who had qualified for a place at a school famous for its music department. 'You absolutely cannot be late. I'm taking you in the car.'

'What about us?' demanded Jess who, like Beth, was hovering beside them in her new school uniform.

'You can walk,' her said mother fiddling with Cormac's tie, 'and Beth can cycle. Just roll down the hill, you'll be there in no time.'

'I'm not walking,' Jess fumed.

'Take the bus then.' Sylvie fumbled in her purse for change.

Beth stomped out of the front door around the side to the garage and her bike.

'Bye darling,' her mother called out of the car

window, while reversing down the drive, but Beth ignored her and glared at Cormac who sat pale beside her in the passenger seat.

The cycle to school was mostly downhill but it was through busy traffic. There were five sets of lights and Beth had to wait for queues of cars to pass. She was tempted to turn around and cycle home again, but what would be the point? There was no one there. In London Gran's warm presence had filled the house like freshly baked buns. Beth shook a tear from her cheek. She must look stupid, crying in her horrible cycling helmet.

Soon she reached a tall grey Georgian building facing the busy main road with a heavy wooden door and St Joseph's Primary written above it. Beth wished she could have attended secondary school with Jess. She would have done so in London – where children entered secondary when they were eleven – but in Ireland Beth was too young and had to wait another year.

She and Sylvie had already been to visit the school,

when none of the children were there. The principal had shown them around the classrooms and playground so Beth knew to wheel her bicycle around the side of the building and add hers to the pile. Slowly she followed a river of children, pushing and shoving each other, inside the building to a room marked Class Six. It was large with windows running along one wall. The children seated themselves at tables clustered into fours. 'Now,' Ms Fitzpatrick pulled a chair out from a table near the front. 'I want you to welcome Beth. She's moved here from London.'

Beth sat down, her face hot. She hoped Ms Fitzpatrick would start talking about something else quickly. A couple of girls at a near bye desk were studying her with cool eyes. The boys were messing too much to take much notice of her.

'Settle down,' Ms Fitzpatrick said. 'Time to take out your homework.' Ms Fitzpatrick was tall and slim. She wore skinny jeans, ankle boots with heels and a pretty floral blouse. She had a dark shiny bob, which swung gently while she was writing on the white-board. During class discussions, children were allowed to shout out, without putting up their hands, which Beth found strange. In her old school, Mrs Green-dale never allowed that. Ms Fitzpatrick seemed to like it. She joked and laughed with them until suddenly she didn't and everyone had to be quiet or they'd be banished to the quiet corner. This happened to a girl called Gráinne, just before first break. She'd been tit-tering and passing notes with the other girls at her table.

'Gráinne.' Ms Fitzpatrick sighed. 'That's enough. Over you go.' She pointed to a corner of the room with a red beanbag and shelves of colourful books. Beth thought it looked like a lovely place to sit but Gráinne flounced and huffed her way there, flopping down with a sulky pout. She then proceeded to study her nails while Ms Fitzpatrick told everyone to tidy up and prepare to line up to go outside for break.

During break-time, most of the girls disappeared

off to the sprawling hockey pitches and tennis courts with arms linked. They had been attending school together for years; friendships were fully formed and they didn't bother about her. Beth discovered that a couple of girls were going out with some of the boys, and a few of them smoked behind the bike shed. There had been none of that in her old school.

Beth wandered outside alone. The playground in her old school was compact and cosy. This playground seemed to have no boundaries at all. If Aisha were with her, they could have walked around together. Beth tried walking alone but felt like a lone tree on an African plain, and so returned to her desk. She took out a dry cheese sandwich. There was no butter or mayonnaise at home, as her mother had forgotten to include it in the weekly shop, and Beth had forgotten to bring a drink, so the dry bread clogged in her throat like cotton wool.

After break it was time for Maths. Beth had always liked Maths and had done these types of sums before.

She found she could do the calculations with ease and, as the week progressed, she realised most of the school work was easier than she was used to. 'Well done, Beth,' Ms Fitzpatrick exclaimed several times. 'Excellent work.' Nearly every day she received high marks and one morning Ms Fitzpatrick read out one of Beth's stories in front of the whole class. 'You really are talented. Well done.'

At first Beth couldn't help feeling pleased. She'd been clever enough in her old school but so were Aisha and a few others. Beth didn't stand out there like she did here. The only subject she couldn't do was Irish. While everyone else read incomprehensible texts full of words, that had weird short lines hovering in the air above some of the letters, Ms Fitzpatrick gave Beth a picture book with Irish words to study, saying, 'You'll pick it up in no time.' Beth wasn't so sure.

After lunch at the end of her first week, Gráinne and her gang trooped back in, and spotted Beth sitting at her desk. 'There's a bad smell in here,' Gráinne said holding her nose.

'Yeah.' One of the other girls giggled. 'I get it too.'

Beth's cheeks burned.

'Sure you haven't pooped your pants?' Gráinne tittered.

Beth focused on the table. It had taken her only a few days to work out that Gráinne O'Reilly was the meanest girl in the class, and yet a cluster of girls swarmed around her like flies around a cowpat. Skinny with messy dark hair pushed off her face with a thick band – like the one Beth's mother wore when cleaning off her make-up – she had very pale skin and wore her uniform short and raggedy as if she were too cool to bother taking care of it.

Beth ignored them. Everyone knew you were supposed to be nice to new children, even if you didn't want to be, but Miss Fitzpatrick mustn't have taught these girls that. Some of them smiled at her briefly but they didn't think to include her and that hurt.

And the following morning, when Beth sat down at

her place, she found the words WE DON'T WANT A NEW GIRL etched into the table with a compass. She glanced around to discover Gráinne staring pointedly at her and her sidekicks smirking and nudging each other. Quickly Beth pulled out her books and pretended to concentrate on what Miss Fitzpatrick was saying but her heart was thudding in her throat. Why were they being so mean? The rest of the day passed in a blur. One girl called, Jane, approached Beth at lunchtime and asked her about where she came from, but Beth was only able to mumble a few words in reply. She couldn't get the words carved into her desk out of her mind. What was she going to do?

After school it was a relief to pant up the hill and return home to the quiet house with her mother reading in the kitchen, and Cormac writing music. Beth slipped into her father's office to Skype Aisha in London. They had arranged to do so by text earlier in the day. Thankfully, since her Gran died, Beth's mother generously topped up Beth's phone credit whenever she asked. Good thing too, as Beth texted Aisha between five and ten times a day.

'So how's everything?' Aisha asked in a breathless voice. Behind Aisha's face, Beth could see lilac walls and posters of Aisha's favourite actors. Aisha must have brought her mother's laptop into her own bedroom. If only Beth could be lying on Aisha's orange duvet with her, chatting together the way they used to.

'Okay. Different.' There was so much that Beth wanted to say but she held back. If she told Aisha about Gráinne, Aisha mightn't understand. She might think her weak and silly not to stand up to her. Aisha mightn't even want to be friends with her anymore. Then Beth would have no one. She couldn't bear that. 'The school work is really easy,' she said.

'Lucky you,' Aisha groaned, 'Mrs Greendale has been piling on the homework this year. It's a nightmare.'

Beth visualised her old sunny classroom and Mrs Greendale's calm voice giving out clear homework that was always checked and corrected the next day. She remembered the classmates she'd known for most of her life. Their lives going on exactly as before. They would be shocked to know that Beth spent her lunchtimes alone and felt such an outsider in her new school. They might not believe it if somebody told them. She hadn't been the most popular girl in the class in London, but she'd always been part of the main gang, involved in everything. Here it was as if Beth had become a completely different person. She didn't know how to get back to the person she used to be.

Aisha giggled suddenly. 'Me and Emily had the best laugh yesterday.'

Beth fell quiet. Aisha talked more about Emily every time they Skyped. Emily had moved to their school a couple of weeks before Beth left, and she and Aisha became friendly when Beth was off from school after her Gran died. Emily was okay, but nothing special, and the more Beth heard about her, the less special she thought she was.

'So we ran home as fast as we could and nobody caught us,' Aisha finished her tale triumphantly.

'Oh right, I'd better go.'

Aisha's tone changed. 'Hey, you okay?'

'Yes,' Beth said quickly, 'of course.' Aisha had never asked her that before.

'You sound different.'

'Okay am I. Problem a you have?'

Aisha giggled, as she always did when Beth talked backwards – it was one of their favourite games. 'Dinner to me calling is Mum. Go gotta I!'

'You see.' Beth croaked. The computer beeped harshly, obliterating Aisha's smiling face and Beth was left alone in her father's messy office. A wave of homesickness swept over her for Aisha's house at dinnertime. Everyone collected around the table: Aisha's two older brothers, one of whom was at university, her sisters, and her father too, always complimenting Aisha's mother on her cooking and asking everyone about their day. As unlike her family's dinnertime as possible.

Beth switched off her father's computer and tiptoed back up to her bedroom.

It was at this precise moment that all of the strangeness began. Beth pushed open her bedroom door and found her books, which she had carefully unpacked and placed on a shelf in order of age – babyish ones hidden near the bottom and more grown up ones at eye-level – had been knocked off and were face down, all over the desk and floor. Her schoolbag hung upside down, her pencil case was open and the coloured feathers, which had stuck out of the heads of her favourite pencils, had been chopped off. She picked up a beautiful pineapple rubber – a present from Aisha that she was saving – teeth marks ridged its jelly edges.

Beth's eyes filled with angry tears. Cormac!

She stormed straight downstairs and burst into the kitchen.

'What?' Jess looked up from stirring something on

the stove.

Beth held out her ruined pencils and rubber. Her chest felt as if it were bursting with an angry balloon.

'Did someone chew your rubber?' Cormac peered at the collection of debris.

'You did!' Beth exploded.

Cormac looked baffled. 'What would I do that for?'

'Because you hate me.'

Cormac paled. 'You're the one who hates me!'

'What's going on?' Sylvie looked up from her papers.

Beth thrust the items under her mother's nose, her hand trembling with rage.

'Oh Beth.' Her mother laughed. 'Did a cat chew them or something?'

Two fat tears dribbled out of Beth's eyes. 'We don't have a cat.'

'Pumpkin.' Sylvie pulled her close. 'I'll get you some new pencils and a rubber.' She swept Beth's fringe aside. 'Will that make things better?'

Beth wrenched herself free. Her mother always suggested things like that but then she forgot or said things like 'not now, darling' if she reminded her.

'Well, there's no need to be like that. Mummy was only trying to help.'

'You've been up there all afternoon,' Jess said. 'You're the only one who could have done it.'

'Why would I ruin my own things?'

Jess smirked. 'Because you're strange.'

Beth scowled at Jess. She hated when Jess acted superior and didn't know how to respond. There was nothing for it but to return and tidy. But Beth wasn't going to forget the incident. No way.

CHAPTER THREE

Early the following morning, the worst thing of all happened:

Beth was brushing her teeth, looking in the mirror, when she noticed her left earlobe peeping out from under her hair. She shouldn't have been able to see her ear; her hair normally covered it and fell all the way down to her shoulder, just as it did on the right hand side. But on this morning her light-brown hair ran in a horizontal line directly above her pink lobe. She threw down her toothbrush and pulled at the stump of hair as if it might extend down like a blind. It didn't.

Someone had chopped off a chunk of her hair while she slept.

She dashed across the landing to Jess's bedroom.

'Go away!' Jess snapped. She was tying her school tie, in front of the mirror.

Beth turned her face to the side.

Jess dropped the tie. 'What did you do that for?'

'I didn't.' Beth fled back to her room.

'Wait!' Jess chased after her.

Tunnelling her face into the duvet, Beth felt Jess's hand on her shoulder. 'What happened?'

'I don't know!' Beth pulled miserably at the stump of hair.

'How can you not know?'

Slowly Beth turned to face her. 'I woke up like this.'

'You can't have.'

'Somebody is doing this to me…' Her head dropped and she began to cry.

'Don't be silly.'

'Yesterday the drawer in my desk was upside down and everything spilled all over the floor. I told you. And my long rubber pencil and my stapler are missing. It's got to be Cormac.'

'No.' Jess shook her head and chewed her lip. 'Cormac's always so busy practising. Why would he do it?'

'He's completely different since he's gone all music

genius.'

'Hang on!' Jess suddenly gasped.

'What?'

'It could be poltergeist!'

'A what?'

'An unhappy spirit.'

Beth stared at her sister with large scared eyes. 'In my room?' she whispered.

'We'd better tell Dad,' Jess said firmly. 'He'll know what to do.'

'But what about my hair?' Beth pulled at it.

'Clip it up.' Jess disappeared and returned moments later with two sparkly clips, with butterflies on them. 'If you pin up both sides, they'll look the same.'

Beth clipped the hair back over both ears and returned to the mirror. She looked about six.

'It looks fine.' Jess assured her.

'Yeah right.' Beth plodded off to school for another day of hell.

It was a quarter to nine when their father arrived

home that evening. 'Lost a foal,' he said shaking his head. 'Don't know why. Perfect little guy, only six months old.' He trudged into the kitchen to wash his hands.

'Kissy, Kissy.' Sylvie pouted her lips at him.

He planted his own lips on hers and she wound her arms around his neck. 'Ugh you're all wet.'

'It's lashing out there.'

'Dad, can we talk to you?' Jess said to his back.

'Give the poor man a minute.' Their mother frowned. 'He's only just got in.'

'It's important, Dad, please.'

'Okay Jess.' His dark eyes locked with his daughter's. 'I'll just get changed.' He winked at his wife. 'See you later.' With a smug smile Sylvie resumed her reading.

'Will I make you a sandwich, Dad?' Jess asked.

'My angel.' He squeezed her arm and lumbered upstairs.

Beth helped Jess make a pile of ham and salad sandwiches (he usually ate at least four) and carried them into the front room. Bill was already there, wearing a clean brushed-cotton shirt and yesterday's crumpled jeans. Beth sat on the arm of his chair and Jess stood before him.

'So, what's up?'

'We think this house has a ghost,' Jess said.

'A what?' He spluttered out a piece of lettuce.

'Go on Beth, tell him.'

Suddenly Beth felt stupid, as if she'd been making it all up.

'Tell him.' Jess urged. 'Go on!'

And so Beth did.

'Where's Cormac?' their father asked, sounding tired.

'He says he didn't do it.'

'What does your mother say?'

Neither of them answered.

'Well?'

'She said it might be a cat.'

He erupted into a laugh, which turned into a rumbling cough in his chest.

Beth fixed him with large anxious eyes but he waved away her concern and took another bite of his sandwich. 'Lock your bedroom door when you're not in it.'

'Oh.' Beth perked up. 'That's a good idea.'

'Right.' He stood up. 'No more worrying. We'll sort this.'

* * *

The next day, much to Beth's horror, her mother turned up at the school gates.

'What are you doing here?' Beth asked. Gráinne and her crew could appear at any moment.

'I came to pick you up. I thought we might go shopping together or something,' her mother said vaguely.

Beth started. 'Why?'

Sylvie ran her hand along the side of Beth's shorn hair. 'Daddy and I feel that we've been overlooking you a bit. You're missing Gran. We all are. And there's all these strange going on in your room.'

Beth tugged on her mother's long purple woollen

shawl. 'Let's go then.' She'd spotted Gráinne coming out of the main door.

'There's no rush. Oh, are they your classmates?'

Gráinne O'Reilly and her band of sour-faced girls were walking towards them, arms linked.

Beth pulled harder. 'No.'

'Weirdo,' Gráinne muttered as she passed them.

'What did she say?' Sylvie asked.

'They weren't talking to us. Come on.'

After a delicious burger and chips in McDonald's, Beth could eat them forever, they wandered around a second hand bookshop while Sylvie talked to the owner (an ancient man, with a large purple nose) about the merits of Shaw versus Beckett. The only children's books Beth could find were hard-backed ones with mouldy old pages and characters who said, 'rather!' and 'spiffing!' every few paragraphs.

'Oh, *The Valley of Adventure*,' her mother said looking over Beth's shoulder. 'I used to love that book.'

Beth knew that. They had it at home, along with

Anne of Green Gables, Little Women and rows of *Famous Five* stories. Beth read them when she had nothing else, but right now she'd love an up-to-date novel about a girl having a horrible time at a new school.

* * *

Later, when they returned home and went upstairs, there was nothing out of place or broken in Beth's room.

'See?' Her mother patted her shoulder.

'What?'

'Perhaps you just needed a fun outing with me.'

Beth shrugged off her hand, and closed the bedroom door. She climbed up on her bed, puffed up her pillows and folded her arms. How dare her mother not believe her? Did she think she was some kind of attention-seeking baby? She tugged at her hair. It still wasn't growing. It wasn't even one centimetre longer and it had been days. Warm tears slid out of the sides of her eyes onto the pillows. What was she going to do? Gráinne and her gang hated her and some of the boys were becoming nasty too. Only the day before Carl O'Toole had called her Weasel. She wasn't sure what a weasel looked like, and didn't particularly want to find out, but she had an idea it was small and rat-like. Of course, she had kept her face rigid to show that she didn't care but the effort was exhausting. Only when she was alone in her room could she let her face relax and reflect the true misery inside.

She pulled the duvet over her head and breathed in. The cover was the same one that had been on her bed in London but it no longer smelled of starch from her grandmother's iron or of the lavender that she used to hang in the hot-press. Instead it smelled of stale biscuits with a hint of rain from having been left out too long on the line. Sighing, she laid her arms down by her sides as if she were dead, or at least how she imagined one might lie in a coffin buried deep under the earth, with worms nibbling on your skin. That's where her grandmother's body was now: under the grass in a graveyard in London, surrounded by high oak trees and old stone walls. Before they left for Ireland, Beth had gone to sit beside the pile of fresh earth and chat to her grandmother, telling her all about the big move to Ireland, leaving school and missing Aisha. And all the while she had done her best not to think of her grandmother's waxen body several feet below but instead imagined her spirit high above, as part of the white wispy clouds, looking down on her and listening.

Thud. 'Aaaaah!' Beth screamed. Something solid and heavy landed on her. She scrambled out from under the duvet. It was a boy. About thirteen years old. He was enormous, all long legs and arms. Beth glanced at the window and the door. Both were closed. She looked up at the ceiling. Where had he come from? 'Get off me!' she screeched and pushed him off the bed onto the floor. Clutching the duvet once more for protection, Beth gasped, 'Who are you?'

Ignoring her question, the boy stood up and walked over to her desk, where he picked up her favourite gold gel pen, and scribbled on the cover of one of her books. 'Smashing!'

'Hey!' Beth jumped up and snatched away the book. 'Leave that alone.'

He had floppy brown curls, cut very short, glittery brown eyes and pink freckled cheeks. His clothes were like something a grown up man would wear: grey flannel trousers and a blazer. Beth couldn't help asking: 'Are you in rehearsals for a play?'

As if she hadn't spoken, he turned to open the drawer of her desk and began rummaging amongst her stickers, pens and pencils.

'Stop it!' She slammed the drawer shut.

'Just looking.' He shrugged

'Leave my things alone.' Her voice shook with emotion. Suddenly he charged past her, jumping onto her bed and bouncing on it as hard as he could. He reached the ceiling with an outstretched hand. 'Yes!'

'Get off my bed!' Beth yelled. Bits of dried mud were crumbling off his boots onto her covers. He jumped once more, very high, and then fell onto the floor where he remained on his knees and seemed to be fumbling with something. Beth walked forward to see. He had matches in one hand. He struck one and held the flame against the wooden leg of her desk.

'What the hell do you think you're doing?' she said in her most outraged voice. She really was outraged, but at the same time she was nervous. This boy was definitely older than her.

He quickly slipped the box of matches into his pocket, oh so casually, as if he hadn't been about to burn her room down. 'Nothing.'

'I saw you with that match. Look, there's a black mark on the leg.'

'That was there before.'

Beth stared at him. How could you argue with a person who lied blatantly to your face?

'You're Beth.'

'How do you know?'

'It's written all over your books.' He pointed at the

shelves.

'Are you some horrible friend of Cormac's?'

'Who's that?' The boy looked interested.

'My painfully brilliant brother.'

'Oh him.' He picked up the calculator on Beth's desk and pressed a few random buttons. 'What's this do?'

'Adds, subtracts and multiplies. Don't you go to school?'

'Course I do.'

'What's nine times nine?'

He picked up a compass and began scratching her desk.

'Will you stop?'

'Don't ask me stupid questions.'

'It's not a stupid question. Nine times nine is eighty-one. See you can do it on this.' She tapped the sum into the calculator and showed him.

'This gives you the answers?' he said amazed.

'Of course. It's a calculator. Duh!'

The boy snatched it out of her hand and shoved it

into his pocket.

'That's mine!'

'Not anymore, it isn't.' He bolted out to the land-ing, slamming the door behind him. She followed him directly but he had completely disappeared.

She checked the bathroom, even behind the shower curtain. He wasn't there. She checked Jess's room, pushing aside the heap of clothes on the floor and searching under the bed – nothing. She opened Cormac's door. He was humming with his back to her, while conducting an imaginary orchestra, and didn't even hear her open the door. Suddenly she heard a loud thud and Beth turned around. The airing cup-board door had burst open and Robbie was splayed on the landing. Quickly he scrambled up and dashed into her room. Beth stood there in shock. Her bedroom door slammed and she heard something heavy being dragged across her room. She sprinted over to open her door but it wouldn't budge. Putting both hands on the door, as if she were pushing a car up a hill,

Beth pushed with all of her might. Inch by inch the door opened and Beth fell into the room. She glanced around. There was nobody there. She checked inside the cupboard and under the bed. The room was entirely empty. Where on earth had the strange boy gone?

CHAPTER FOUR

'I've found out who did it.' Beth grabbed Jess the second she came in from school.

'Did what?' Jess dumped her schoolbag in the hall and sighed. She was always bad-tempered after school.

'All that stuff in my room. It's a boy who wears really weird clothes. He came tumbling into my room out of nowhere and he isn't a ghost – he left big huge footprints on my bed cover. Look.' Beth dragged her upstairs to her bedroom and pointed at the soiled duvet. 'There.'

Jess wrinkled her nose. 'Ugh!'

'I caught him trying to set fire to my desk. He's mental!'

'How old was he?'

'Twelve or thirteen.'

Jess peered out of the window. 'Maybe he lives on the road.'

Beth stood beside her and they both gazed at the houses opposite. In the one directly across from them, lived two men, both of whom wore suits and drove big fancy cars. At the weekends they walked to the shops together with their dog. Next door was an old lady and beside her a married couple with a baby.

'Or he could live behind us. Maybe he hops over the wall into the garden.' A glint came into Jess's eye. 'We could lay a trap for him.'

'What kind of a trap?' Beth asked eagerly.

'I'll have to think about it.' Jess said darkly and sauntered off to her bedroom.

* * *

That night Beth barely slept. She was going to get her own back on that boy and Jess was going to help her. It was the most exciting thing that had happened since leaving London.

The next afternoon Jess announced her plan: 'I'm going to stay in the kitchen and you do your homework in the hall. There's only two doors into this house and he's got to come through one of them. If mystery boy comes over the back wall, I won't miss him.'

But by six o'clock nothing had happened. Jess poked her head into the hall. 'Are you sure you saw him?'

'Of course I did. I want my calculator back.'

'Well, I give up,' Jess said. 'I'm going upstairs.'

'We can't let him get away with this!' Beth pleaded.

'Let me know, if you catch him.' Jess heaved her school bag on to her shoulder and plodded upstairs. 'I'm doing my homework.'

Beth decided to give up also. Feeling deflated and disappointed, she trudged up to her bedroom. Once there she opened the drawer in her desk and retrieved an old blunt knife she'd stolen from the kitchen. Kneeling down in the corner of her room, she used it to carefully lift up a floor-board under which she kept the one thing about Dublin that gave her solace. It was her secret.

One of the workmen had noticed the loose floor-board when he was painting her room. 'Eh, look what

I found,' he said pulling out a small brown notebook.

Beth put out her hand. 'May I have it?'

'You may,' he handed it over, 'but if you find a secret code in there I want to be in on it.' He winked at her.

There were no secret codes but there was something infinitely better: the diary of a girl named Dorothea Montgomery who was eight years old, but from her writing Beth would have guessed her to be much older – or maybe children were able to write better in those days. The diary was dated 13 April sometime in the 1950s. The last number was an ink splotch and Beth couldn't read it. Every day Beth read a little. Dorothea's diary was the closest thing she had to a friend in Dublin and she savoured every word of it.

13th April

Today is my eighth birthday. Mummy and Daddy gave me this diary. I'm going to write in it every day and I'll hide it so no one will ever find it. Mummy and Daddy gave me paints and brushes. I'm going to make a picture of Marmaduke sleeping in his bed.

Robbie made me a card this morning. It said: 'Dere Dort, Hapy Birtday, Robbie.' But yesterday morning he put bricks up the exhaust pipe of Dad's car and when Dad was going to work, the engine cut out and made a huge bang. Robbie laughed like it was the funniest thing he ever saw, but Dad looked like he was going to cry. Robbie was sent to bed without supper, again. I secretly gave him two cold sausages, a potato and a slice of apple tart, but I doubt it was enough. Poor Robbie, he's always in trouble.

14th April

Robbie spilt a whole bottle of milk all over my watercolour sketch of Marmaduke. I've dried it out, but it still smells horrible and Marmaduke looks nothing like the regal cat he is. I won't be able to give it to Dad for his birthday. Why is my brother so difficult?

Beth closed the diary. If Dorothea was eight in the 1950s that would make her in her seventies today – the same age as her grandmother had been. Was Dorothea still alive and could she ever find her? Suddenly

Jess came onto the landing and Beth quickly stashed the diary under the floorboards. If Jess knew about it she would want to read the diary too, and Beth wasn't ready to share it yet.

Jess popped her head in the door. 'Sure you didn't imagine him?'

'NO!' Beth glared at her. Why did no one believe her, listen to her, or take her seriously?

'Well, let me know if he turns up.' Jess smirked and strolled away again.

Beth was determined not to give up. She would prove Jess wrong. Maybe if she hid in her room she could catch him in the act. Yes! Instantly she clambered into the old cupboard that had belonged to her grandparents. It was a perfect hiding place. Lucky Beth was small and managed to fit inside. The floor was hard and she hugged her legs to her chest, resting her chin on her knees. Through the chink of the slightly open door, she could see the end of her bed, one corner of her desk and her schoolbag leaning against it. She must have been sitting there for twenty minutes. Her eyes were beginning to close when she heard something. What was it? She leaned forward and peeked through the crack in the door. That was when she witnessed something completely impossible. All by itself, her school bag lifted off the ground. Beth blinked, rubbed her eyes and looked again: now a pair of scissors was cutting a line across the bottom of the bag making a great gaping hole in it. With a bang, her copies and books fell on to the floor in a heap.

'Wha...?' Beth watched in utter amazement.

The bag dropped on top of the pile and the scissors landed on top of the bag. Then the chair at her desk swivelled around in a circle.

But there was nobody in it.

Beth clutched her legs tighter, barely daring to breath. If only Jess were with her.

Suddenly she heard a voice at the door. 'Beth?'

Beth was too terrified to answer.

'Where are you?'

The chair came to a standstill.

The cupboard door creaked open and Jess stood frowning down at her. 'I was calling you.'

'Look!' Beth whispered, pointing at the mess on her floor.

Jess took in the raggedy school bag, books and scissors. 'What happened?'

'It did it all by itself.'

'What?'

'I saw the whole thing. And there's someone sitting in that chair.' Beth pointed at it.

'Yeah, right.' Jess plonked herself down in the chair.

'It must have moved.' Beth glanced around the room.

'Come on, Mum said she's taking us to the cinema.'

'But we can't! There is a poltergeist... you were right.'

'Be—eth.' Jess drew out her name and wouldn't listen. 'I'm starving. Come on!'

Protesting, complaining and pleading Beth was

dragged downstairs to the kitchen. By the time they arrived she began to wonder if she'd imagined the whole thing. Had her black school bag really been hovering in mid-air, and had a pair of scissors cut the bottom of it? Could it really be true?

Beth sat down in the kitchen cold and shaky. Sylvie was opening rectangular tinfoil cartons of food. 'Spaghetti Bolognese, Tagliatelli Carbonara and plain Spaghetti Napoletana, for you Beth.'

Beth let the mixture slop onto her plate. Ever since Gran had died they'd been eating take-away dinners every second night. Aisha had been hugely envious of this when she came to dinner. 'We never order in at home,' she gushed when Sylvie asked if she'd like Indian, Chinese or Italian.

Beth didn't think it was anything to be envious of. By the time take-out meals arrived they were often cold and after a while nearly all of them tasted the same – no matter what you ordered. She much preferred dinner in Aisha's house. There was the smell of spices, pretty earthenware bowls of rice and delicious sauces that Aisha's mother laid on the table before the whole family. Everyone was collected together. In Beth's house her mother ate on the sofa, while reading, Cormac ate at the piano, with the plate at one end while his free hand tinkered with notes, and her father often sat in the office frowning at something on the computer screen. Jess usually watched T.V, with the meal on her lap, but if she had prepared dinner herself, which she sometimes did after a particularly inspiring home economics class, she settled herself at the kitchen table, where Beth sat with a book.

That evening they took their usual perches, except for their father who wasn't home yet, and then all went to the cinema together where Sylvie bought bags of bitter sweet jelly squirms, boxes of popcorn and large fizzy drinks. The film was a period drama in which the women walked around in long dresses with their chests sticking out. Cormac begged to see the latest animated thriller instead: 'No, darling. You shall sit with us. That film will be full of horrible children. I don't want you getting the flu.'

Beth didn't see or hear anything of the film. What was she going to do? Could she tell her father what happened? Would he believe her? Should she ring Aisha? She glanced at her mother who was staring at the screen in a trance. One thing was for certain – there was little point in talking to her.

If only Granny were still alive. She'd have believed her. Banishing thoughts of her smiling grandmother, Beth bit into a squirm letting the bitter sugar fizz on her tongue. She'd just have to hide in the cupboard again, and somehow get proof.

During the long film, she had an idea. What if she recorded the spirit? Everyone would have to believe her then. Beth didn't know whether her phone camera would be able to record unearthly beings. Maybe the spirit would be able to sense the camera and not appear, but if she could just make a recording of her schoolbag hanging upside down all by itself. Who wouldn't believe her story then?

CHAPTER FIVE

A t a quarter to four the following afternoon, Beth settled herself in the cupboard with her mother's phone fully charged and pointing through the open crack in the door. By a quarter to five, the left side of her bottom was numb and one of her legs had gone to sleep. She clicked the camera off to save the battery. A minute later she turned it back on. It would be just too unlucky to have it switched off the moment something happened.

Then something did happen: the chair at her desk sank down on its spring and turned, all on its own, to face the bed. Quick as she could, Beth pressed record.

The chair became perfectly still. She shuffled her numb bottom closer and manoeuvred the camera lens between the crack. The pillow on her bed was indented as if a head were resting in it, but Beth hadn't lain on her bed since she had made it that morning, and that pillow had been perfectly puffed up when she came home from school. She zoomed in on the pillow even though it wasn't exactly convincing evidence. She could imagine Jess's sneer and her mother's bemused expression. She might even ruffle her hair saying: 'My dreamer.' Beth hated when she called her that.

Suddenly something flew across the room. What was it? She shifted her weight from one numb bum cheek to the other. Oh no! The chair was moving again, swirling in circles. This was it. She pointed the camera at the chair and her prayers were answered. Through the lens she saw something pink flying towards her. Closer it came, the colour becoming more intense, blocking out the light, until all she saw was pitch darkness. She moved her eye from the view-finder to find her pink pyjama bottoms hanging over her phone. Losing her balance she tumbled out of the cupboard, onto the floor. 'Ow!' The phone fell out of her hands and her right cheek landed on something curved, hard and rough like the toe of a boot. But all she could see was the pale-blue carpet. She reached out a hand. There it was again: hard, heavy and most definitely there. The invisible boot had a thick rim around each side. She felt the crisscross of laces, above that a soft sock and then – the unmistakable feeling of warm flesh.

'Ah!' she snatched her hand away. Suddenly the boy was sitting beside her in the chair.

'How did you get there?' Beth sat up amazed.

'I was here all the time.' He sniggered.

'Where did you come from?'

'My house.'

'You weren't here a minute ago.'

'Neither were you.'

'Yes, I was.'

'In the cupboard?' the boy peered into it. 'Ugh!' He waved a hand. 'Your gym shoes stink.'

'Shut up!' Beth slammed the door closed behind her. 'Where do you live?'

'3 Hawthorn Road. Not that it's any of your business.'

'Don't be stupid. I live in 3 Hawthorn Road. You can't.'

'I do.' He picked up a four-coloured biro and began taking it apart. 'And so does my mother, my father, my older brother and my kid sister, Dorothea.'

Beth had to sit down. Wasn't Dorothea the girl who wrote that old diary she'd found under the floor?

Beth looked up at him. 'What's your name?'

'Robbie.' She was beginning to feel dizzy. Dorothea was always writing about her brother, Robbie. This boy couldn't be the same person, could he? It was impossible. The diary was written over sixty years ago.

'What's your brother's name?' Beth asked quietly.

'Jack,' he said with a scowl.

'And do you have a maid called Mary?'

'Yeah.' Robbie looked up.

'Oh God.'

'This is wizard.' Robbie held up the broken pen.

Coming out of her daze Beth snatched it off him. 'I'm going to tell my sister you're here.'

'Oooh. I'm SOOO scared!' He stuck a thumb in each ear and wiggled his fingers on either side of his head.

It was most unlike her but Beth hurled his school cap onto the ground and grabbed a hold of his blazer.

'Oooow!' He roared, his face becoming redder. 'Get off!' He pushed her away.

'No.' Her hands clamped on. Robbie jumped onto the bed dragging Beth with him. Then, all of a sudden, the strangest thing happened; Beth felt as if she were being sucked into a vacuum cleaner. Her cheeks were squashed in, her hair felt as if it were going to be ripped out of her scalp, and her whole body was pulled, pulled, pulled. She wanted to scream, but there was not one scrap of air in which to draw breath.

Then thankfully it stopped.

'Get off!' Robbie yanked his jacket out of her hands.

'What the...?' Beth stared around open-mouthed. She was standing in a dark kitchen, more like a corridor than a room, and there were two women at a wooden table. One, small with a wizened face, was chopping potatoes and plopping them into a pot of water. The other, plump with pretty dark hair curled closely against her head, was grating cheese into a bowl. Both women lifted their heads. 'Oh Robbie,' said the plump one. 'Where have you been?'

'Nowhere.' Robbie stuck his hand into the pot and grabbed a raw potato.

'Leave that alone!' called the older woman.

'Can't catch me!' Robbie ran through a door and slammed it behind him.

Beth remained against the wall breathing as quietly as she could. Couldn't these women see her? She was only a couple of feet away.

'He's getting worse.' The pretty one sat down on a rickety wooden chair. 'What am I going to do with him?'

'Ah, Isabelle,' the older one nodded. 'Maybe he'll grow out of it.'

'We said that when he was five.'

'Well, thirteen-year-olds are notoriously bad.'

'Why can't he be more like Jack?'

'Ah, but there's not many like your eldest,' Mary said with a misty expression. 'And he's nearly eighteen.'

Suddenly the younger woman cocked her head like a bird. 'Oh goodness! Is that Ron home?' She hurriedly wiped her hands on her apron and washed them under the tap. 'I haven't even done my hair.'

'You go and tidy yourself up. I'll finish up here.'

'Mary, you're an angel.' She pulled open the kitchen door and called out: 'Ron, darling!'

Beth watched her go. Still the older woman didn't seem to see her. Maybe she had bad eyesight.

'Here we go!' she grunted, heaving the huge pot of potatoes onto the range behind her. While her back was turned, Beth took her chance and tiptoed through the door into the hall. Where on earth was she? Had she and Robbie squeezed through the wall to next door's house? No, that couldn't be right. Mrs Porter's hall was cluttered with odd pieces of furniture and things left out to give her grown-up children whenever they came to visit, which wasn't often. This hall was bright and smelt of furniture polish. There was a vase of pink roses on a gleaming side-table by the wall.

'Shepherd's pie for dinner, darling,' Beth heard coming from the front room.

'Lovely, Isabelle,' a pleasant male voice replied.

Beth looked up the stairs. Robbie had to be up there. Should she go up? Normally Beth wouldn't dream of creeping around someone else's house uninvited, but if Robbie didn't observe rules of normal decent behaviour why should she?

Beth put her weight forward onto the first step. Oh no! It creaked, exactly the same way as the first one did at home.

She waited a moment but nobody appeared in the hall and so she continued up the stairs. They curved around towards the front of the house, the way they used to in her house before they knocked down the back wall, so they could build her parents a large bedroom overlooking the back garden.

At the top of the stairs she paused on the landing. Here she was faced with six closed doors: two on her left, two straight ahead and two on her right. She stepped to the left first, where Cormac slept in her house, and gently pushed open the door. There she saw a boy, or was it a man, sitting at a desk. He had black hair smoothed down with some sort of gel, that made it look wet, and he was wearing a jacket, that reminded her of the type of thing her father wore out to the theatre.

Mercifully he didn't move and Beth quietly pulled the door closed. Next she tried the room to her far right. There was a young girl, a few years younger than Beth, lying on a bed.

'Oh!' Her body shuddered in fright when the door opened.

'Oh God, I'm sorry,' Beth said, blushing to the roots of her hair. 'I'm looking for Robbie.'

The girl rolled slowly off the bed, and tiptoed to the

door. She peered about the landing, ignoring Beth. 'I know you're there, Robbie!' She giggled.

The girl looked up at the ceiling. Beth glanced up too. What could she be looking for up there?

With one final check the girl closed her door, leaving Beth alone on the landing.

As an experiment, and because this girl didn't look the least bit scary, Beth opened the door again.

'Hi,' she said standing directly in front of her.

'Robbie!' The girl scampered off her bed and grabbed the door handle. 'Do you have invisible thread?'

'No, it's me,' Beth said boldly. 'I opened it.'

The girl flounced back to her bed. 'If you're not going to tell me, leave me alone.'

'Okay then.' Beth returned to the landing. She decided to try the door straight ahead which in her house would lead into her bedroom. There, sitting at a wooden writing desk and digging a compass needle into it, was Robbie.

CHAPTER SIX

'This is where you are,' Beth said.

Robbie continued digging another letter into the wood, completely ignoring her.

'You shouldn't have left me in the kitchen.'

Robbie was exerting so much pressure that the needle of the compass broke and he hit his hand hard against the table. 'Ouch!'

'I'm talking to you,' she snapped.

He shook his sore hand and held it against himself. 'DOROTHEA!' he roared at the wall.

'What?' The girl from next door arrived.

'Get me your compass.'

'You already broke it.'

'Well, get darling Jack's then.'

'Nooo!'

'Tell him you need it to do your homework.' Robbie sucked his knuckle.

'He won't give it to me.'

'He will if you turn on the tears.'

She sighed, and trudged across the landing. Beth watched her knock on the door of the older boy and quietly go inside.

Robbie leaned back in his chair with his hands clasped over his stomach and stared at the ceiling.

'You're horrible,' Beth said to him. 'You're even worse than my brother Cormac, and I didn't think that was possible. You're a bully, a liar and a thief!' As she remembered all the pranks he'd played on her, she became more indignant. 'You don't deserve a sister like Dorothea, or your mother, who cooks you dinners and worries about you.'

Robbie took absolutely no notice.

Feeling angrier than she could remember, Beth scanned his room for something to throw. There was a narrow single bed, neatly made, with a puffy quilt on top of the blankets. There were two shelves holding broken model aeroplanes, bits of wire, a toy car with wheels missing and tubes of overflowing glue. Next she spotted a jar of something black on the desk, right in front of him. The word Quink written on the label.

Quick as a flash, Beth snatched it off the desk, twisted off the lid, and poured the contents over Robbie's head. Black liquid dripped down his pale face creating uneven inky black and white stripes.

'What the blazes!' he spluttered.

Beth grabbed one of the model aeroplanes off the shelf and hurled it onto the floor. 'You ruined my school books and my bag.' She grabbed the toy car and ran to the window but she didn't know how to open it: it wasn't like her window at home which opened outwards, this window had a bar of wood in the middle, a nail and a washer which was too stiff to unscrew.

'Gimme that!' Hands tugged at her jumper, and started moving upwards around her chest.

'Ugh, get off me! You creep!' Her hand caught him on the chin and cheek.

'I knew it was you,' he said looking at her properly

for the first time.

'Well done, Einstein.' Beth twisted her jumper back into place.

'Don't EVER touch my planes.' Robbie carefully picked up the delicate construction from the floor, as if it were an injured bird.

'Only if you stop sneaking into my room and breaking everything. And leave my books alone.'

'I bet you don't even read them,' he said through gritted teeth. 'I bet you're only showing off!'

'If I find one more thing broken in my room, I'll smash your stupid planes into smithereens.'

'What are you doing here?' Robbie asked crossly.

'I don't know. How did we get here and why were you ignoring me?'

'I didn't know you were here,' he said gruffly.

Beth gaped at him. 'You are such a liar –'

Robbie interrupted her, 'You're not visible until you touch someone.'

'Huh?'

'That's how you got to see me in your room. Because you felt my leg.'

'I did not!' Beth said hotly.

Robbie smirked. 'You were lying on the floor. Remember? And you felt your way up my ankle.'

'Oh yeah.'

'No one had been able to see me before that.'

'Well, I'm sorry I spoilt your fun.'

Robbie scowled. 'Go home now.'

As if he hadn't spoken, Beth marched to the window and peered out. The street looked almost exactly the same as her one. It was on a slope and the houses had the same peaked roofs, bay windows and redbrick arches over the front doors, but there were some differences. There were no tarmac driveways in which to park the cars: these houses had perfectly neat green lawns instead. Also the house opposite had a yellow wooden door instead of a white PVC one and its windows were different.

There was something else that was odd. Beth looked

at her watch. It was five fifteen in the afternoon. The street should have been crammed with traffic queuing to get out onto the main road.

'Where am I?'

'My house,' he said without looking up.

'Yes, but what road is this.'

'Hawthorn Road. I told you.'

'This can't be Hawthorn Road!'

'Go down to the end of the street and check the signpost.'

Beth glanced out of the window again. A woman was walking by, wearing a long beige coat, and a woollen hat like a turban. She was pushing a huge pram with wheels, like a bicycle. Who pushed their baby around in something like that?

Beth pressed her nose against the glass and spotted a car parked in the driveway below. It had a high domed roof, and thin wheels with white hubcaps.

'What sort of car is that?'

'Morris Minor.' Robbie stood beside her at the

window. 'I'm going to drive that.'

'You can't. You have to be seventeen.'

'Not if you drive off road,' Robbie said loftily.

Just at that moment there was a knock at the door and Dorothea stuck her head in. 'Who are you?' She stared at Beth. 'Why is she wearing trousers?' she asked Robbie.

'They're tracksuit bottoms,' Beth informed her.

'Don't worry about her.' Robbie said. 'She's going home now.'

'Suits me,' Beth said trying not to sound hurt. 'Now, if you'll just tell me how to get out of here –'

'Why, through the door, of course, silly,' Dorothea said surprised.

Beth looked at Robbie who grinned smugly, his arm around Dorothea, the picture of the perfect brother.

'Right then.' Beth strode onto the landing.

'Good luck!' Robbie waved with a grin.

She glowered back at him. Where could she go? Not out onto that strange street. No. She'd return to the kitchen. It was where she had come from after all.

Beth retreated down the stairs, pushed open the door to the kitchen, and walked inside.

'Can I help you?' The older woman who'd been oblivious to Beth before, stared at her, potato masher in mid-air.

'Eh … I'm Beth.'

'Yes?'

'And... Robbie brought me.'

The woman nodded grimly. 'Oh, he did, did he?'

'The thing is, I'm not sure how to get home.'

The woman's eyes moved up and down Beth's body, taking in her school tracksuit and runners. 'What school do you go to?'

'Saint Joseph's.'

'That's a boy's school.'

'Well, they take girls too.'

'That's the first I've heard of it.'

'I only joined a couple of months ago. I've moved here from England.'

'Ah.' The woman put the potato masher down. 'And how do you know our Robbie?'

'He's been coming around to my house in the afternoons.'

'So that's what he's been up to.'

'Yes.' Beth walked over to the part of the wall, where she first found herself. There was no door. Absent-mindedly, she ran her hand along a hair-line crack at eye level.

'What you doing?' the woman asked. 'You wait there, I'm going to get….' But Beth didn't hear what the woman was going to get because her voice became faint and then inaudible. She was experiencing that sensation again, like a machine sucking the fat out of her body. There was a rushing in her ears, and a heavy weight pressed down on her chest making it impossible to breathe. She swirled upside down and around, as if she were on a violent ride at a fun fair. Eventually she was spat out in a heap onto what she thought might be her own bed. Yes, there were the faded ink spots on the corner of her duvet and her bookshelf was facing her, filled with its many comforting titles: *Inkheart, Skulduggery Pleasant*, the full series of *Harry Potter*, and loads of Jacqueline Wilsons.

She was home.

Beth scurried to the window and gazed outside. The street was packed with sleek shiny cars, driven by single passengers, some talking on mobile phones, waiting for the lights to change. She even heard Cormac doing his wretched scales downstairs. But she was observing the street from exactly the same angle as she had seen it from Robbie's room. It didn't make any sense.

CHAPTER SEVEN

Beth thundered onto the landing and flung open her sister's door. 'Is there another road that looks exactly like this one?'

'Get out!' Jess screeched. She was standing in her underwear and had obviously been gazing at herself in front of her long mirror. Beth ignored her and rushed onto Jess's bed.

'What are you doing?' Jess grabbed a towel and wrapped it around herself.

Beth told her story as quickly as she could, barely stopping to breathe.

'So, you're telling me, that you squished through a hole in the wall, into this phantom boy's house, and then you squished back through it here.'

'It was more like sucked.'

'For God's sake!' Jess pulled a jumper over her head with one hand, while keeping the towel wrapped around her torso with the other.

'In Robbie's house this is Dorothea's room and across the landing is his older brother's, Jack.'

Jess turned to face her. 'Listen Beth, stop making all this up. You're not the only one here who's miserable, you know.' Jess pulled on her jeans. 'It's no fun for me either. I've got to do all the cooking, and I've loads of homework, and I've no friends and I'm never going to have a boyfriend,' she blurted.

'Course you will,' Beth said stunned. 'You're gorgeous.' It was true. Jess was as tall as their father, with long shiny black hair and big Bambi eyes. She looked like a model when she wore her tiny shorts and backcombed her hair into a high pony tail.

'Yeah, say Mum and Dad.' Jess rolled her eyes. 'They don't count.'

At least they told Jess she was attractive. No one ever told Beth she was gorgeous. Gran was the only one who had ever told her that she was pretty and that was only when she smiled, 'which you should do more often,' she used to say.

'Come with me to Robbie's house.' Beth met Jess's eyes in the mirror.

Jess sighed. 'I don't have time. I've two tests tomorrow and a project to do. Get Cormac to join in your games.'

'NO!' Beth slammed the door and stomped back to her room.

Flinging herself back on her bed, she stared at the ceiling. When they first moved in, it had been a musty yellow colour with dark bits along the edges, but when the extension was built the whole house had been freshly painted white. Now new spiders' webs had collected in the corners and she spotted a faint crack running along the plasterwork that she had never seen before. Her eyes followed it to the edge where it curved and continued down the wall by her bed. She sat up. The crack was about as thick as a single strand of hair and reminded her of the crack in Robbie's kitchen – the one she had rubbed her hand along, before she suddenly found herself home again.

Was that how Robbie did it? By rubbing a crack in the wall?

She reached out a hand to touch it, but then quickly pulled back. Her arms and legs were still limp from being sucked through the last time and she wasn't sure she had the energy for all that again, just yet.

She lay back down, folded her arms across her chest and battled tears. She hated Jess, acting all superior, in her secondary school uniform. They used to be friends. They used to do stuff together, but that was before Gran became ill. Jess had been allowed into the adult loop, but Beth hadn't. Jess had been told how serious their grandmother's illness was; she'd been warned. The first Beth had heard about it was when she came home from a sleep over at Aisha's and it was all over. It was only later that she'd realised they'd sent her away on purpose, so that she'd been out of the way when her grandmother died. Jess had known about that too.

She hated Cormac too, of course, but most of all

she hated Dublin. Nothing was going right. Gráinne O'Reilly had to be the most horrible person ever born. Recently she'd laughed at Beth's English accent, when Beth had been forced to answer a question in class, and had nick-named her 'Queenie'. And when Miss Fitzpatrick handed back a corrected homework, delightedly informing the class that once again Beth had achieved top marks, Gráinne grabbed Beth's hair at break-time and hurled her around in a circle. Gráinne's group of cronies jeered and egged her on. Beth had to run to keep up and when Gráinne finally let go she had a hefty clump of Beth's hair in her fist. The others only laughed. The rest of the children were too far away in the playground to see what had happened.

Beth returned to the classroom, her scalp stinging. Nothing like this had ever happened in her old school. Mrs Greendale would have packed Gráinne O'Reilly off to Junior Infants until she learnt how to behave. Miss Fitzpatrick was kind but she was usually busy correcting a huge pile of copy books or helping some-body else in the classroom. Beth didn't know how to tell her.

And now Beth was lumbered with this pesky boy, Robbie, to make her life even more difficult. If only Gran were still here. She was the best grandmother, but instead of wearing a grey bun, like they had in picture books, she had soft curly hair that was sometimes purple depending on how recently she'd been to the hair salon.

'What should I do, Gran?' Beth whispered into her empty bedroom. Of course, there was no reply, only the sound of traffic on the main road. Beth squeezed her eyes tight shut and imagined that she was back in her old home in London. She used to love lying in bed, listening to Gran going up and down the hall, early in the morning or late at night. It made her feel safe. She snuggled down under the covers and imagined that her grandmother was in the house with her. She saw her opening the door, coming into her room and sitting on the bed beside her. She could almost smell the fragrance of her grandmother's face cream – it smelled like sweet peas – and feel her neatly ironed woollen jumper.

'Gran,' Beth whispered.

'Yes, Beth.' Her grandmother patted her shoulder. 'I'm here.'

'Oh Gran.' Tears seeped down her cheeks. 'Is it really you?'

'Yes, it's me.'

'I hate school and I hate living here and we never have any nice dinners anymore.'

'Well, Jess is doing her best.'

'She never talks to me.'

'That's because she's so busy. If you helped Jess more in the kitchen, I'd say she'd find more time to talk.'

'Oh.' Beth paused. She'd never thought of that. 'She doesn't believe me about Robbie. I don't know what to do.'

'Pay that boy back,' came her grandmother's no-nonsense reply. 'Give him a dose of his own medicine.'

Beth jerked in her bed and concentrated hard. What else would Gran say?

'Go back through that wall, and mess up that boy's room. No one should be allowed to get away with what he's done to your things.' Gran laid a gentle hand on Beth.

Beth stayed very still. She didn't want to break the spell.

'Beth, you're a strong and clever girl. Don't you forget that.'

'I don't feel strong. I—'

Suddenly the bedroom door opened and Jess walked in. 'Who're you talking to?'

'No one.' Beth quickly dried her eyes.

Jess looked about. 'Don't tell me,' she said sarcastically, 'it was the vanishing boy.'

'No, it wasn't!' Beth snapped. 'What do you want?'

'I want you to peel the carrots. I've done the potatoes and I need to finish my geography homework.'

Beth was about to object, but then remembered her grandmother's words, 'If you helped Jess more in the kitchen, she'd find more time to talk to you.'

'All right.' Beth slid off the bed.

'Oh!' Jess looked surprised.

'Only because I've nothing else to do,' Beth said grumpily.

'Gee thanks!' Jess rolled her eyes and strolled back into her room.

Alone in the kitchen, Beth began the task with little pleasure. The carrots were knobbly and the water was cold. So much for having time to talk with Jess. She studied the walls while her hand fumbled in the sink for another carrot. Robbie had said he came through the kitchen. Had he meant his kitchen or hers? She couldn't see any crack in the immediate vicinity. Mind you, he had probably lied. He nearly always did.

CHAPTER EIGHT

Beth had little time that week to experiment with squashing through a crack in the wall. Her father was off sick from work with the flu, and she and Jess took it in turns bringing him hot drinks. Their mother spent all day at rehearsals in The Gate Theatre. 'It's a world premiere,' she told them. 'We might even take it to Broadway.' She giggled excitedly, tying a fluffy purple scarf around her neck.

'Do you know anyone else who has a mother like ours?' Beth asked Jess when she was gone.

Jess shook her head. 'No one.'

'Sometimes do you wish she was just normal, you know, like other mothers?'

'Who wants an ordinary mother? The girls at school know she's an actress and they think it's brilliant.'

Beth didn't say anything. Nobody knew Sylvie was an actress at her school. She didn't tell them anything.

On Saturday morning their father got out of bed and said he was going into the surgery.

'But you're not better yet,' Beth said worried. 'You're sick.'

'Don't worry, pet,' he wheezed putting on his socks and shoes, 'I'm grand.'

'But you have a temperature.'

'I'm a lot stronger than I look and the surgery won't run without me.' He clumped downstairs to get his all-weather jacket and boots from the hall.

'What'll we do?' Beth asked Jess.

She shrugged. 'He must be better otherwise he wouldn't be going, would he?' Jess looked at her watch. 'I'm going to a school hockey match this afternoon.'

Beth swallowed down panic. Jess was making friends at school and she still had none. 'Do you want to come on a bit of an adventure first?' she asked.

'What sort of an adventure?' Jess eyed her warily.

'A surprise. It won't take long. Come on.'

'Where are we going?'

'My room.'

'How exciting,' Jess drawled.

'It will be.' Beth dragged Jess into her room. 'Right, get up on the bed beside me.'

'Take off your shoes!' Jess screeched.

'Oh, yeah.' Beth flung her runners onto the floor. Jess carefully undid the buckles of her black leather shoes and stepped up on the bed beside her.

'Now what are we going to do?' Jess took hold of Beth's hands. 'Bounce?'

'No. Run your hand along this crack in the wall.'

'What?' Jess let go of Beth. 'This is stupid.'

'Here, hold onto me,' Beth said huffily, 'I'll do it.'

'God, Beth, I worry about you.' But Jess gave Beth her hand.

Taking a deep breath, Beth rubbed her free hand along the crack backwards and forwards. Please let this work, please let this work.

It did.

'What the—?' Whatever Jess was going to say was

lost in a whooshing noise like a tornado sucking them faster and faster into its centre. There was no air to breathe and just when Beth thought her lungs were going to explode from pressure and lack of oxygen they arrived into the kitchen in Robbie's house, just like before.

'Where the hell?' Jess wrenched her hand free.

'Robbie's house,' Beth said with a smug smile. 'Told you.'

'But you said –'

'Shush, someone's coming.' Beth became very still. 'But they shouldn't be able to see us.'

'Whaaa—' Beth put her hand over Jess's lips just as a tall boy of about seventeen came into the room. He was the one Beth had seen upstairs. This time she could see his face. He had a large nose and dark eyes. He walked to a cupboard, and took out a glass pot of opaque honey. Then he grabbed a large spoon from a drawer and dipped it into the pot.

Jess raised two questioning brows. Beth smiled. He

twirled the spoon, lifted it to his mouth and, with one hand underneath to catch the drips, strolled out of the room.

'Who is he?' Jess breathed the second he had gone.

'Jack. The one I told you about.'

'Jack,' Jess said dreamily. 'He's gorgeous.'

'God, you'd fancy anyone. Come on. I'll show you Robbie's room.'

Jess followed her eagerly to the kitchen door.

'Remember, they can't see us, but if you touch someone they will. Be careful.'

'Okay.'

The hall was empty and there was no noise coming from the front room.

'It's cold here.' Jess rubbed her upper arms, looking at the rickety side table and daintily upholstered chair in the hall. 'Hey, look at the retro phone!' Sitting on the table was a black, heavy-looking telephone with a handle sitting across the top of it and a circular dial.

'Leave it. We're going upstairs.'

They creaked their way up the stairs. 'Robbie's room is here.' She pointed at his door.

'And Jack's?' Jess looked at the other doors.

'That one.' Beth sighed, pointing at his door.

'Well, you go into that crazy boy's room. I'm going in there.' Jess tweaked her long ponytail to make it higher and rubbed her lips together.

'You're supposed to be coming with me.' Beth pouted.

Jess shook her off. 'Let me have some fun.' She tip-toed across the landing and pushed open the older boy's bedroom door.

'Who's there?' Robbie's older brother turned in his chair to look out onto the landing. With her finger on her lips, Jess slunk into his bedroom. 'Stop fooling around, Robbie.' Jack sighed and kicked the door shut again.

Beth stood alone on the landing; she may have lost Jess but that didn't mean she couldn't go through with her plan. Gran had told her to mess up Robbie's room and she would, starting with his precious planes.

She pushed open his door to find Robbie on his bed with Dorothea beside him. She was crying. 'Why can't you be good?' Dorothea was sobbing.

Robbie's chin was jutting forward like Cormac's did when anyone interrupted his music. 'They won't send me to boarding school.'

'But mum said –'

'I'll run away,' he said sulkily.

'But then they'll send you even further away.' Dorothea wailed. 'England!'

'No, they won't!' Robbie scowled.

'But Robbie –'

'STOP IT!' He shoved her away from him, and Dorothea scurried out of the room, still crying. Beth stood quietly watching Robbie on the bed. It was the perfect opportunity to break something but it didn't seem right to mess up his room now. She'd never seen an older boy cry before. Cormac had done it heaps of times, of course, but he was only a baby.

'Robbie?' she said. Her voice sounded loud in her own ears but he didn't hear. She took a few steps into the room and sat down on the bed.

He rubbed his nose and eyes, and looked up.

Beth leaned away from him.

'It's you, isn't it? Don't wriggle away from me.' He jumped up.

Beth thought for a moment and took a step directly in his path. Bang! One of his hands landed splat on her cheek as he walked straight into her. 'Knew it!' He stared at her.

'So you can see me now?'

'What you doing here?'

'I came for a visit, you know, the way you visit my room?'

'Well, you can go home.'

'Why are they sending you away?'

'None of your business.' He turned back to the bed.

'Tell me or I'll come back in the middle of the night and stamp on your plane.'

He whipped around. 'You wouldn't.'

'Would.' Beth stared resolutely back.

His glittery brown eyes scrutinised her but Beth held strong. It seemed to work. Eventually Robbie slumped on the bed. 'If I don't pass my exams, they're sending me away.'

Beth sat down on the little wooden stool beside him. 'Why wouldn't you pass your exams?'

He kicked the leg of her stool. 'The teachers say I'm stupid.'

'And what do you think?'

'I know the answers but they don't give me enough time to write them down, and I can't spell the stupid words.'

'Show me.'

'No, you're only a girl.'

'Yeah, and girls do better in school.'

'They do not. Girls are pea-brains!'

Beth followed Robbie's eyes to a leather bag in the corner. She stalked over to it.

'Don't touch that!'

But she had already opened the flap – it was very like Cormac's precious music bag – and pulled out a copybook with Robbie Montgomery Inlish Comperhsenson, written on the cover. She flipped open the first page and gazed at the messiest muddle of words she'd ever seen.

'Give it to me!' He lunged at it.

'No!' Beth ran out onto the landing with Robbie chasing after her.

'For God's sake!' Jack burst out of his room onto the landing. Beth saw Jess standing behind him with a silly grin on her face. 'Who are you?' He stared at Beth confused.

'A painful girl!' Robbie tried to snatch his copybook from her but Beth stuffed it up her jumper. That didn't stop him; he grabbed her in a rugby tackle and the two of them fell onto the floor.

'Robbie!' Jack pulled his brother off. 'Leave her alone!'

'You're not stupid!' Beth cried.

'Give it here!' Robbie snarled.

'You're dyslexic.'

'Dis –what?' Jack asked.

'Dyslexic.'

'Shut up!' Robbie grabbed the copy off her.

'Stop.' Jack took a firm hold of Robbie's jumper. 'Say sorry to this girl.' Robbie squirmed under his brother's grip. 'Go on!'

'He finds it difficult to read and he gets his letters muddled up,' Beth panted. 'My friend, Aisha, is the same.'

'What are you talking about?' Jack asked.

'She knows what's wrong with Robbie?' Dorothea's quiet voice emerged from her room.

'Yes, I do.' Beth turned to her gratefully. 'We'd loads of people with dyslexia in my old school. They learn in different ways. That's all and they need extra help in school.'

'NO, I DON'T!' Robbie yelled.

'It doesn't mean you're stupid. Aisha's one of the cleverest people I know.'

'Who's Aisha?' Dorothea asked.

'My best friend.'

Jess sidled across the landing to Beth. 'Let them see me,' she whispered.

'Not yet,' Beth said.

'Not yet?' Jack asked confused. 'What are you talking about?'

'She's bonkers,' Robbie said pleased.

'When are they sending you to your new school?' Beth asked, ignoring Robbie's remark.

'As soon as he gets his exam results,' Jack said in a resigned voice.

'Right.' Beth grabbed Jessica's hand. 'We've got to go.'

'Hey wait!' Jack, Robbie and Dorothea all stared at Jess in amazement. 'Who's she?'

'Oh, my sister Jess.'

'Hi.' Jess smiled directly at Jack.

'But where did she come from?'

'Can't tell you.' Beth pulled at Jess. 'But we'll be back!'

Beth dragged Jess down the stairs and into the dark kitchen. Quickly she found the crack, rubbed it and the two of them swirled around like the spin programme in a washing machine until they landed in a heap on Beth's bed.

'What the hell did you do that for?' Jess rubbed her sore arms and legs. 'Why did we suddenly have to go? What do you do with the wall again?' Jessica peered at it.

'You rub your hand along this crack.'

Jessica reached out her hand. 'Which crack?'

'But don't do it now!' Beth pulled it down.

'Why not?'

'Cos we can't return yet. I've stuff to do first.'

'I don't care.' Jess turned back to the wall.

'Don't Jess. This is my secret.'

'Oh for God's sake.' Jess rolled her eyes.

'We'll go back soon. I promise.'

CHAPTER NINE

That night Beth message Skyped Aisha on her father's computer.

How can I help someone who's dyslexic but they don't know it?

Is this 'someone' a boy or a girl?

A boy.

Oooooh! LOL!

He's thirteen and completely deranged.

How do you know he's dyslexic?

He can't spell and he fails all his exams, but he knows loads of stuff.

Funny his teachers haven't copped.

Yeah, I know.

Tell him to ask the special needs teacher to give him a test.

I don't think he'll want to do that.

How to you know him?

He's a neighbour.

The boy next door. LOL!

Beth heard her father coming in from work.

Got to go. Dad's home.

Okay. Chat soon. xxx

Bill Boffin appeared at the door, flushed and coughing.

'Will I get you some tea?' Beth asked.

'Lovely.' He held onto the doorframe for support.

Beth walked into the kitchen. Her mother was lying on the sofa by the window, reading by the last of the daylight.

'Do you want the light on?'

She looked up, cheeks flushed, 'Oh thanks, Pumpkin,' and returned to her book.

Beth filled the kettle, flicked the switch on and gazed out of the window at the outline of bushes and trees in the garden. Suddenly it struck her – she didn't want Robbie to be sent away. It was funny to admit it, but she actually liked him. He'd looked so forlorn on his bed, and it wasn't his fault he'd dyslexia. It must be so frustrating not to understand what it was. It was no wonder he was always in trouble. And, without doubt, Robbie was the most interesting thing that had happened since moving to Dublin. Without him to distract her, horrible Gráinne O'Reilly would take up even more of her headspace, and the less she thought about her the better.

'What's the big sigh for?' Sylvie asked as she dropped her finished novel onto the floor.

'Nothing.'

'Nothing Schmuthing.' Sylvie patted the space beside her. 'Tell me.'

Beth walked over, her stomach tightening.

'Is it Gran?'

'No.'

'What then?'

The kettle clicked off and Beth turned back to it.

'You used to tell me everything.' Sylvie pouted.

Beth tried to remember a time when that was true,

but failed. Gran was the person who listened. Mum often forgot what you said moments later.

'Jess is the same, too busy for her own mother.'

Beth filled her father's mug with hot water. His was the largest in the house. Beth and Cormac had given it to him when they used to club their money together to buy joint presents at Christmas.

'Can I've a cuppa too?' Sylvie shifted to make herself more comfortable on the sofa.

Beth took her mother's mug from the cupboard. 'Diva' was written on it in large bold letters. Her agent had given it to her.

'Thanks, darling.' Sylvie wrapped her long slender fingers around the mug. 'What on earth is wrong with you? I don't know what I'm going to do with you.'

Beth stared at her mother. She'd often witnessed fans flock around her after performances telling her she was marvellous. And she was – when she was on stage – she would do anything; even scrub a floor if the role demanded it. But off stage, her mind was always somewhere else.

'It's just, everything is different.'

'I know.' Sylvie sighed. 'You've had a lot to put up with.' She reached for Beth's hand.

'Schools' hard.'

'Those girls outside the school?' Sylvie raised an eyebrow.

Beth nodded, surprised her mother had noticed.

'There's always people like that.'

'Are there?'

'Yes, and do you know what?'

'What?'

'They're usually very unhappy themselves. I remember a role I played –'

'Eh, I'd better bring Dad his tea.' Beth backed out of the room. Once her mother began talking about a role, it went on for a long time. She padded into the study where she found her father with his eyes closed and head leant back against the chair.

'Dad?'

No response.

'Dad?' She poked his shoulder.

'Uh?' He jerked forward. 'I was gone there.' He blew his nose and rubbed his eyes, which were red and watery. She sat on the arm of his chair and he put one arm around her waist to hold her beside him. 'You okay?' he asked.

'Hmmm…' She fiddled with her sleeve. 'I kind of miss Aisha.'

He squeezed her hand. 'What about at school? Is there anyone half way decent there?'

'Nope.'

'You know,' he said. 'I moved schools when I was your age, and it took me until after Christmas to sort out who the all right ones were.'

'I'm not friends with Gráinne O'Reilly.'

'What's she like?'

'Horrible.' Beth's throat hurt.

'Well, you send her along to me for a big fat injection. I'll sort her out.'

Beth couldn't help smiling. 'What did you do about the nasty ones in your class?'

'I ignored them if I could, and if I couldn't I got my own back.'

'How?'

He leaned his head back to think, but something caught in his throat and he became gripped by a coughing fit.

Beth fell off the arm of his chair. Her father choked for air. 'Daddy, Daddy!'

But he waved her away, seized by the irritant in his chest.

'Mum! Mum!' she called. His chest sounded worse than ever: rumbling like the engine of a ship.

'Darling,' Sylvie called from the kitchen, 'it's alright. He's been coughing like that for weeks.'

'No, you've got to come!' Beth burst into tears.

Sylvie arrived into the study to find Bill Boffin lying on the floor, gasping for air.

'Oh my God!' Sylvie fell down beside him. 'Beth,

call an ambulance.' She cradled his deathly pale head in her lap and asked if he was okay but Bill Boffin's face was turned away. He had lost consciousness.

* * *

Half an hour later, her father was carried out of the house, on a stretcher.

Sylvie tugged at the ambulance men. 'What's the matter with him?'

'Best get him to the hospital, Ma'am. They'll sort him out.'

'No!' Beth cried desperately. 'Not hospital!'

'They've got to.' Sylvie grabbed her coat and speaking to Jess, who was standing on the stairs, said: 'Don't let anyone in.'

Jess nodded dumbly.

'Daddy's going to be alright.'

'How do you know?' Beth sobbed.

Sylvie gave Beth an absentminded pat. 'Jess, take care of your sister and brother.'

The ambulance moved off slowly, its blue lights

flashing and bouncing off the neighbour's wall. Beth listened to the siren until it faded into the night.

'Stop crying, Beth,' Jessica pleaded. 'Daddy's going to be all right.'

But Beth couldn't. She went into the front room and shut the door behind her. What if he died in hospital? What if she never saw him again?

Jess followed her in. 'You're freaking Cormac out.' Her brother sidled in behind her, the vertical line between his pale brows more pronounced than ever. 'Stop, please.'

But Beth's body had begun to shudder uncontrollably.

Jess wrapped a blanket around Beth's shoulders, but the shaking didn't stop. 'Are you hungry?'

'No,' Beth and Cormac answered at the same time.

'Let's do something to keep our minds off things.'

Cormac glanced at the piano. 'I could practise my scales.'

'No. Something together. The three of us.' Jess nudged Beth and jerked her head in the direction of upstairs.

Was she talking about going to Robbie's house? Beth couldn't believe it. How could Jess even think of it?

'Come on.' Jess stalked out of the room, and Cormac reluctantly followed, as if he didn't want to.

Beth threw off her rug and raced to the door. 'What if Mum rings? We'll need to be here to answer.'

'We won't be long,' Jessica called down from the landing. 'Now, are you coming?'

Still trembling, Beth hurried up the stairs. There was no way they were leaving her behind on her own.

CHAPTER TEN

Over an hour later, when Beth, Jess and Cormac tumbled home flushed with excitement, Sylvie charged into Beth's room. 'WHERE WERE YOU?' she roared. 'WELL?'

'How's Daddy?' Jess asked in a breathless voice.

'We're not talking about Daddy. I asked, 'Where were you?''

Cormac looked at Beth, who looked at Jessica, who looked down at her feet.

'And why aren't you wearing any shoes?' All three of their shoes were on the floor by Beth's bed.

'We took them off,' Cormac said nervously.

'Why?' Sylvie put her long hands on slender hips.

There was a long silence.

'What is it? What's going on? I demand to know.' Sylvie's voice rose several octaves. 'Jess?'

'We went out.'

'In your socks?'

'We went to someone's house,' Beth mumbled.

'How come I didn't hear you come in? Do you know how worried I've been? I return from the hospital to find the house completely empty. No note.' She dropped onto the chair and hid her face in her hands.

'Sorry Mum.' Jess stepped off the bed and stood beside her mother.

'A boy lives near here,' Beth ventured.

'What boy? I don't know any boy.' Sylvie wiped her nose with the back of a hand.

'His name's Robbie.'

Sylvie gazed at her three children, her eyes red from crying. 'Don't you know how sick your father is?'

'Is he very sick?' Jessica asked.

'It's pneumonia.'

'Will he die?' Beth whispered.

'No, he won't die.' Sylvie pulled Beth to her chest. 'But he'll have to stay in hospital for a while.'

The four of them were silent as the information sank in.

'So he won't be going to work,' Cormac said eventually.

'No.'

'What will happen to the practice?' Jessica asked.

'I suppose we'll have to get in a locum.'

'Dad won't like that.'

'Well, that's what's going to have to happen. Dad needs to get better.' Sylvie took a deep breath, pushed back her shoulders and attempted a smile. 'Now off to bed. There's school in the morning.'

* * *

More than ever, the next morning, Beth didn't want to go school. If Gráinne O'Reilly said one mean thing, which of course she would, Beth would not be able to keep her face rigid and Gráinne would have won. She peaked over her blankets and noticed that one of her gel pens was writing, *Im here*, on her homework notebook.

She sat up. 'Don't touch me,' she said into the empty room.

Dont wont to appeared on her notebook.

'My Dad's in hospital.'

The gel pen didn't move.

'He's been coughing.'

The chair by her desk sank by an inch or two.

It was strange to be voicing her worries to nobody, but somehow Beth found it easier than if Robbie were visible. It was almost like talking to herself, or Gran.

'And if I go to school Gráinne O'Reilly will be there.'

Hus Grawnya

Beth frowned. 'She the nastiest girl I've ever known. Everyone thinks she's really cool but she hates me.'

The chair swung around in a circle, then the gel pen wrote: *Let me cum to skool Il poo in her bag*

Beth began to giggle. 'And you could put a spider down her top.'

Grate sho me the way

Beth felt excitement rising in her. 'Okay but wait

here. I've to have my breakfast.'

Get me sum

'Right. I'll meet you at the front gate in ten minutes.'

In her hurry, Beth bumped into Jessica in the bathroom.

'We shouldn't have stayed so late,' Jessica whispered. 'I never thought so many people would fit into our front room.'

'I know,' Beth remembered Robbie's mother playing the piano while a tall smartly-dressed man sang beside her and about twenty people stood squashed in a semi-circle, holding glasses of dark red liquid and eating tiny white sandwiches.

'Pity Jack wasn't there.' Jessica sighed. 'Hope he doesn't have a girlfriend.'

Beth stared at her. 'You can't go out with him.'

'Why not?'

'He lives in another time zone!'

'We don't know that.'

'Yes, we do. They've no T.V, they call the radio, the wireless. They've no calculators or mobile phones.'

'It doesn't matter.' Jessica shook her hair. 'He likes me and I like him.'

'You're crazy.' Beth left the bathroom and skipped down the stairs for her breakfast.

CHAPTER ELEVEN

Transporting Robbie to school wasn't easy. He sat on the saddle, without touching her, while Beth stood on the pedals leaning forwards away from him. Luckily, most of the journey was downhill but it was difficult to keep them both steady. Even though he was invisible Robbie weighed a lot.

When they arrived at the school bicycle-shed, and Beth leaned her bike on top of other ones, one of the larger bikes lifted up and cycled down the street all on its own. It looked so strange, like something out of a movie. 'Come back!' Beth screamed. The bicycle turned around and hurtled back up the street, skidding to a halt beside her. Beth could imagine Robbie chuckling as he threw it on top of the other bikes. 'Right, follow me!' Beth led him towards the class-room with her head down – if she avoided Gráinne's eye, there was usually less trouble.

'Hi, Queenie,' Gráinne called the moment Beth entered the room. 'Love the hair.' She tittered with one of her sidekicks. She then opened her mouth to say something else but the chair she was sitting on, suddenly pulled out from under her and she fell backwards onto the floor. 'Ouch!' she yelled.

Beth pressed her lips together to stop herself from smiling.

'Who did that?' Gráinne scanned the room.

'It wasn't me,' timid Jenny Walsh squeaked.

'Me neither,' Rebecca Forrester added quickly.

'Gráinne O'Reilly, sit down.' Miss Fitzpatrick entered, her hair gleaming as usual.

Gráinne gave one last sweeping glare around the room and moved to sit down, but just as her bottom was about to reach its destination, her seat was whipped away once again. She fell down harder this time; Beth heard the impact of the hard floor shuddering through Gráinne's skinny frame.

'Gráinne!' Miss Fitzpatrick exclaimed. 'Get up!'

'But I didn –'

'Stop being silly!'

Gráinne rubbed her bottom, hobbled over to her chair, and with her hands on either side of the seat, carefully sat down. Her brown eyes studied each classmate, but when they met Beth's, Beth stared innocently away.

Miss Fitzpatrick returned to the top of the classroom saying: 'Time for Engl—' but she got no further as there was a loud bang, followed by a yell, as two of Miss Fitzpatrick's whiteboard cleaners slammed against Gráinne's ears, and dropped to the floor.

The class sniggered.

'Who?' Gráinne gazed around, and for the first time Beth saw fear in Gráinne's eyes.

'Gráinne, I don't know what's got into you this morning, but whatever it is, stop it!'

Gráinne ignored Miss Fitzpatrick and glared at Beth who was by now openly grinning, 'I'll get you!'

Feeling unusually courageous, Beth made the 'whatever' shape with her two thumbs and index fingers. Gráinne's mouth dropped open while her sidekicks, Fiona and Karen, gazed at Beth in awe.

Class continued as usual until break time, however when the bell went and Gráinne stood up, she took one step forward, then tripped, and fell violently against the back of a chair. She clutched her stomach and groaned.

'God, Gráinne, what'd you do that for?' Fiona tittered, unsure whether Gráinne was playing one of her jokes. But Gráinne was gasping for air, and her eyes were darting about the room like a frantic animal.

Karen pointed at Gráinne's Converse runners. 'Some one tied her laces together!'

Everyone edged forwards to see. It was true. The polka-dot laces of Gráinne's pink Converse shoes were tied firmly together.

'Who did that?' Fiona asked.

'Dunno.' Karen was dumbfounded.

Beth almost felt sorry for Gráinne, but then she

remembered Gráinne swinging her in circles around the yard and pulling out clumps of her hair.

'Are you sick, Gráinne?' Fiona suggested innocently.

Gráinne shook her head, shivering and still rubbing her stomach.

'Maybe she's got her period,' Karen whispered dramatically.

'Help me!' Gráinne growled through gritted teeth.

'I'll undo your laces.' Karen hurriedly knelt beside her.

When Gráinne was eventually upright she lunged forward like a boxer. 'When I find out who did this...' she panted.

Beth backed out of the room and scurried away to find Robbie. The most probable place was the bicycle shed. Sure enough, when she arrived, the brakes on one set of handlebars were squeezing in and out all on their own. 'I can't believe you did that,' she whispered. The handlebars stopped moving. 'It was brilliant.'

When the bell went, she hurried back to class.

Robbie remained outside so Gráinne experienced no more trouble for the rest of the day.

That afternoon, they cycled home together and slipped up to Beth's room. Robbie grabbed her hand for a second and then appeared sitting down by her desk. 'I'm going to come back tomorrow,' he said gleefully. 'Just wait and see what I'm going to do to your teacher.'

'No, not tomorrow. I want to go to your school,' Beth said.

'No,' he replied stubbornly. 'There's no point in us going there.'

'Yes, there is,' she said with determination. 'I'm going to sit your exams.'

'What? But you're only a gir–'

'If you say that again, I'll hit you.' She clenched her fists.

Robbie was silent, for a moment, as if he were considering her suggestion. 'I go to Sandford Park.'

'So?' Beth knew the school. It was a private

fee-paying one near her house.

'It's for boys only.'

'Girls go there now.' Beth had seen them trailing in and out of the gates.

'They do not!'

'Do too. Anyway, I'll be invisible, remember.'

Robbie moodily kicked the leg of her desk. 'It won't make any difference. You won't be able to do my work.'

'Ugh!' Beth shot angry breath out of her nose. If Robbie weren't so good at tormenting Gráinne O'Reilly, she'd have punched him by now. 'I don't have to know the answers. I'll be your scribe.'

'My what?'

'You tell me the answers and I write them down.'

'Really?' A glimmer of hope shone in Robbie's eyes.

'Yeah, it's normal. Loads of dyslexics have scribes for exams.'

That night Beth lay awake making plans for the following morning. She would have to forge a sick letter from her mother to get the day off school, then stick the note under mother's nose. That would be easy: her mother would sign anything. Beth snuggled down under the covers with a smile. Tomorrow was going to be fun.

CHAPTER TWELVE

The next morning, while lying in bed not fully awake, Beth absentmindedly experimented by rubbing the crack in the wall. The next minute she found herself hurtling into Robbie's kitchen before she meant to. It was eight o'clock and Robbie and his family were having breakfast in the dining room. Beth could hear them talking and the chinking sound of cutlery against plates. She followed Mary, the maid, carrying a dish of sausages in to them.

Robbie's older brother, Jack, was tucking into two boiled eggs, toast, rashers and sausages. The smell made Beth dizzy with longing. Robbie munched two eggs, toast and several rashers and sausages. Dorothea sipped at some milk and nibbled a bowl of porridge. 'Can Abigail come to tea, Mummy?' she asked quietly.

'Of course she can, darling.' Robbie's mother buttered a slice of toast and placed it on Dorothea's plate.

'Just make sure Mrs Hetherington knows.'

'I will.'

'What time is Abi coming?' Robbie looked up.

'Swallow first, then speak.' His mother frowned.

'You're not to play tricks on her,' Dorothea said anxiously.

Robbie sniggered and began humming.

'Remember Robbie, best behaviour.' His father lifted his face from behind a newspaper, and Beth recognised the good-looking man with the moustache who had been singing at the party. 'You're on your last chance.'

Robbie's face flushed and he muttered something inaudible.

Beth shivered. She wore no shoes or socks and was still in her fleece pyjamas. She should really go home to get properly dressed but Robbie's mother was fussing around, asking if anyone would like more tea or hot milk, and Beth was longing to answer, 'Yes,' and sit down and join them. She'd never seen such a generous breakfast. When everyone had finished eating, there were two left over rashers in a dish in the centre of the table. If only she could have them.

'Exams begin today,' Robbie's father said. 'Are you prepared?'

Robbie didn't answer and Beth imagined how he might be feeling. Aisha said it had been horrible when she hadn't understood why she couldn't pass exams as easily as everyone else. 'I thought I was stupid but then I was tested and Mrs Greendale explained that it was just because my brain processes information in a more complex way to most people, so it takes longer. I didn't feel like such a freak anymore.'

'I hope you're going to make us proud.' His father reached out and touched Robbie.

'Yes, Dad,' Robbie mumbled.

'He will,' Dorothea said nodding at her father.

'Let's hope so.' Robbie's father folded his paper and stood up. 'That was delicious, Isabelle.' He gave his wife a kiss on the cheek. 'I'll see you later.'

'Can I get a lift?' Jack stood up.

'Of course you can. Tell me about that new bike of yours on the way.' The two of them left the room chatting amiably. Robbie's mother and Dorothea followed shortly afterwards and Robbie was left alone.

Quick as a flash Beth grabbed a rasher.

'What the—?' Robbie glanced about and quickly closed the door.

Beth touched his hand. He stepped away glancing at her pink fleece pyjamas and bare feet – which were now blue – sticking out the bottom.

'My school uniform.' She giggled.

'Very funny.'

'What time do you leave?'

Robbie looked at his wristwatch. 'Now.'

'You can't. I've got to go home and get changed.'

'Too late.' Robbie grinned.

'Wait!' Beth ran to the kitchen, and rubbed the crack until she felt herself being sucked inside. Moments later, she tumbled onto her bed and knowing there was no time to change slipped her bare feet into runners, and grabbed a puffa jacket off the back of a chair.

In under a minute she was back in Robbie's kitchen, where Isabelle and Mary were clearing up the breakfast dishes.

'It'll be good drying today,' Mary said looking out of the window.

'I hope so,' Isabelle peered out too.

Beth saw the door into the hall was open and so she slipped out to the street, just in time to see Robbie disappearing around a corner. She chased him along the pavement and onto the main road. It was not easy to keep up – Robbie's legs were much longer than hers – but eventually he slowed down when he met some boys also dressed in grey trousers and blazers. Their hair was cut very close to their heads and they looked much neater and cleaner than the boys in Beth's class, but their behaviour was no different. They jostled against one another, pushing and shoving. Robbie was easily the tallest of all of them. Beth noticed how he glanced behind him intermittently but, of course, he couldn't see her and so she slowed down to catch her breath. That's when she realised how quiet the road was. It was like Christmas morning, or walking along a country lane. Any car that happened to trundle past looked like one from the black and white films Gran used to watch, and many of the houses Beth expected to see weren't there. Instead green fields lay on either side of her, filled with cows, sheep and horses. Mature trees lined the road and the air was unusually fresh.

She was so enjoying the sweet birdsong and country atmosphere that she almost missed Robbie and his friends turning into the gateway of the school. The drive way led through pretty woodland up to the property, which had two peaked roofs and Tudor style cladding over red bricks. The windows were long with wooden frames, and there was a balcony over the entrance. It reminded Beth of houses in posh parts of London. A swarm of boys, all dressed in blazers, were piling up the steps into the main entrance. Keeping her distance, Beth followed.

Inside the main door, Beth shrank between two rows of wooden lockers and watched the boys surging pass. They seemed terrifyingly loud and she was very grateful to be invisible.

Keeping a steady eye on Robbie, Beth joined the avalanche of running feet, making sure not to touch anyone or let them touch her. Pulling her puffa jacket tightly around her, she slipped into Robbie's classroom, just after a rather messy boy who was fumbling with his school bag. The room was cold and dim, with a fire burning in the grate. A collection of wooden desks faced a larger desk at the top of the room. Beth smelled old leather, dust and something else that she didn't recognise. Furniture polish? No teacher was there and the noise was escalating – most of it coming from a group at the back of the room. Robbie and another boy were using chairs to fence with one another. A circle of boys was cheering them on.

Then a sudden whoosh announced the arrival of the

teacher, making Beth jump.

'SIT DOWN!' he roared. Standing tall and forbidding in his black cape, he reminded Beth of Professor Snape from Hogwarts.

'Montgomery,' the teacher barked, 'what did I just say?'

Robbie gave the other boy one last jab, and flopped down at his desk.

'Tests.' The teacher waggled an armful of papers. 'You'd better have been studying.'

'Yes, Sir,' a couple of voices assured him.

'Good.' He walked briskly about the room, his cloak flapping behind him like batman. 'You have an hour to complete this, and it's very important.' His eyes zoned in on Robbie.

Robbie glanced away. He sat in the back row on a wooden bench clamped to the desk by thick metal arms. His knees were forced wide apart, jutting out either side of the desk, making him look trapped.

'Work in complete SILENCE.'

Beth tiptoed between the desks to Robbie who had turned the paper over and was gazing at it forlornly.

How was she going to help him? She couldn't sit on his knee – not that she'd particularly want to – as she'd materialise the moment they touched. Her only option was to stand behind him and peer down at the paper. It was a geography test.

Question one: List the twenty-six counties in Ireland.

Robbie had written Dulbin and Wiklow, and was attempting a third county. It was taking him ages. At this pace, he'd never finish the questions on time.

Beth fumbled in her jacket pocket for a pen. Yes, there was one there from school yesterday. She knelt down beside Robbie's desk and turned his exam paper towards her. Robbie jerked back in his seat.

'What is it, Montgomery?' The teacher looked up from his notes.

'Nothing, Sir.'

'Good. We both know this is your final chance.

There's no place for a duffer like you in Sandford Park.'

'Yes, Sir,' Robbie muttered staring at his examination paper which had words emerging like invisible ink: whisper the answers and I'll write them down. Beth noticed Robbie suddenly smirk. He knew she was there.

Robbie began murmuring the counties into his collar: Wexford, Waterford, Cork and Kerry. Beth didn't know them well, as she had studied British Geography in London, but did her best to spell them correctly. She guessed it wouldn't matter too much if they weren't perfect. She wrote as quickly as she could and waited for Robbie to read the next question which involved filling in Irish Mountain ranges and river on a map. After what felt like ages, Robbie pointed at a river and said, 'Barrow.'

'Who's talking?' the teacher barked. 'If I catch anyone cheating, they'll be expelled. Hear that Montgomery?' He glared at Robbie who kept his head down, cheeks flaming.

As quietly as possible, Robbie pointed at places on the map and whispered the names of mountains and rivers. It was almost impossible to get close enough to hear him without touching and Beth found herself looming over him like a weeping willow.

Question number four was an essay on the life of a river. Beth had never studied that topic in class but Robbie seemed to know all about it. He began whispering urgently about rivers beginning as streams high up in the mountains, then meandering along flat planes and ending up in the ocean. Beth began scribbling away, quite enjoying the exercise and learning loads. Who knew rivers were so fascinating? She had written two full pages and was reaching for a third when she realised they had run out of paper.

Resisting the urge to dig Robbie in the ribs, she wrote in large capitals NEED MORE PAPER!

'Uh?' Robbie frowned at the message.

HURRY! They were already twenty minutes into the exam. She felt like kicking him, but of course she couldn't. But she could poke him with his own pen, and she did, right in the middle of his hand.

'Ouch!' Robbie jumped.

The teacher's eyes peered over the tops of his glasses. 'One more squeak out of you, Montgomery, and you'll be out on your ear.'

'Yes, Sir,' Robbie said furiously.

GET PAPER! Beth wrote on the last available space on the page.

After several moments, Robbie got up from his seat, walked to the top of the classroom to retrieve several blank sheets of paper off the teacher's desk.

His teacher raised a brow. 'That's a first.'

Robbie wisely said nothing and returned to his desk. Immediately Beth continued transcribing all of Robbie's instructions, and the more she wrote, the more it became obvious that Robbie was very clever indeed.

When time was up, the teacher strode up and down the aisles collecting the tests. As he picked up Robbie's pages, his face clouded with suspicion. 'You've been studying?'

'Yes, Sir,' Robbie said innocently.

'Well, let's see if you can keep this standard up. It's going to take more than one good Geography test.' He turned on his heel and flapped back up the classroom.

Everyone began shuffling out of their desks and Beth squashed in as close to Robbie as she dared, but it was no use, a boy from the desk behind knocked into her as he passed.

'What's this?' he said staring at Beth's hair, black puffa jacket and pink fleece pyjamas. 'Are you a girl?' he asked stupidly.

Beth glanced desperately at Robbie.

'She's my cousin,' Robbie lied.

'What's she doing here?'

At this point several other boys turned around to see what was happening.

'How did you get in here?' A boy with thick-rimmed black glasses peered at her.

'Eh…through the door?' she answered.

'When?'

'Just now when the bell went.'

'No bell rang,' said a tall boy with red hair.

'Well, before that.'

The boys formed a semi-circle and gaped at her as if she were an exotic animal.

'Have you never seen a girl before?' Robbie said crossly.

'Not like that one, no.' One of them laughed.

Beth blushed and pulled the jacket tighter around her. 'I came to see Robbie,' she said in a high voice.

'Ah!' A knowing glint came into the boys' eyes. 'She's your cousin, right.' One of them winked at Robbie. 'What if Speccy finds her?'

'He won't,' Robbie said firmly. 'She's leaving.'

'No, I'm-'

'Yes. You. Are.' Taking hold of an elbow, he escorted her into the corridor. 'Move!' His long legs could make much larger strides than Beth's and she had to trot to keep up with him.

'Hey, Montgomery. Who's the bird?'

'Wouldn't you like to know?' Robbie faked a smirk and manoeuvred Beth into an empty classroom.

'Robbie!' Beth faced him. 'All that stuff you said about rivers. It was brilliant!'

Robbie let go of her arm. 'No, it wasn't.'

'It was! I bet you'll get best in the class.'

'But I didn't write it myself.'

'It doesn't matter. It was all your ideas. You know loads!'

'You think so?' Robbie didn't know where to look. 'Eh…why are you helping me again?'

'Because…' Beth stuttered. 'Well, I…'

'You… what?'

'I don't want you to go to boarding school. I want you to stay so you can keep getting back at Gráinne for me,' she blurted.

'That skinny girl in your class?'

'Yeah.' Beth became rosy under her freckles.

'Why don't you just give her a hard time the way

you do to me?'

'Dunno.' Beth paused to wonder about it. 'You just bring out that side of me. You're so annoying.' But it was more than that. Robbie provoked something within her in that no one else ever had. She was different with him to how she was with anyone else: feistier, angrier, and more carefree. With Robbie she felt like her true self.

'Has no one ever taught you how to fight?'

'No,' Beth said nervously.

'I've trained Dorothea.'

'You have?' Beth couldn't imagine tiny, timid Dorothea fighting anyone.

'Yeah,' Robbie chuckled. 'No one goes near her now.'

Beth spread her feet into a wide stance. 'Go on then.'

'Not now! I've got my next exam in twenty minutes.'

'What'll I do?'

'Stay here.'

'But what if somebody comes in?'

'Hide in here.' He opened a large wooden cupboard.

On one side shelves were packed with papers and chalk and on the other paintings were piled on top of each other.

'I can't stand on those!'

'You will, if someone comes along.'

'But Robbie –'

It was too late; he'd marched out of the room on his long legs.

CHAPTER THIRTEEN

eth rubbed her stomach. It was mid morning and the effects of two rashers had long since worn off. Everyone said school food was horrible – and in the 1950s it was probably worse – but right now Beth would eat anything. She wondered what Robbie was having in the canteen.

After what felt like at least an hour, Robbie returned.

'What took you so long?' Beth said grumpily.

'I had to eat. I can't do an exam on an empty stomach.' He rubbed his belly.

'Well, come on then. Let's get it over with.' She moved towards the door.

'You can't go out there again.'

'Why not?'

'You're visible!' He rolled his eyes. 'And you say girls are cleverer than boys.'

'Well, how are you going to pass your English?'

'I'll manage,' he said gruffly. 'You'll have to wait here. Don't go running back to my house. My mother will have a fit if she sees you. She doesn't approve of girls who wear trousers.'

'Huh?' But Beth had no time to question further as once again Robbie left the room.

This time the wait was far worse. The lining of her stomach ached. She developed a headache, and was horrendously thirsty. According to her watch it was three o'clock when he reappeared. Most of the boys seemed to have already left.

Robbie entered looking cross. 'Come on. The back way out should be clear.'

Her legs were in cramps from folding up inside the art cupboard and it took a while for her to disentangle herself.

'Hurry!' Robbie tugged her arm.

They sprinted along a corridor and down a couple of steps into a cold dark room filled with wooden seats and desks piled one on top of each other. Beth could see cobwebs gently swaying and imagined spiders hiding in corners. She shivered. 'Hey, what's that?' Beth saw a glove, and three sticks in a pile.

'The wicket.'

'Wicket?'

'Do you not know anything?' Robbie refused to explain any further and, with backs bent, they crept out of the building, and onto the front grass.

'Into the trees.' Robbie pulled her behind a trunk, and they stood facing each other, Beth's face level with Robbie's chest. She could smell the washing powder from his clean shirt. 'Don't move!' Robbie instructed as a teacher came around a corner, his cloak flapping like a huge black pelican about to take flight. 'Wait until he's gone.' When there was no one in sight, Robbie pulled her out just as suddenly. 'Now, when we get home, go around to the back of the house and wait in the garage.'

'All right.' Beth rubbed her arm crossly.

Waiting in the garage was far worse than the cupboard. It was freezing cold and there was a smell of oil coming from a motorcycle leaning against the wall. 'Sneak me something to eat!' Beth pleaded as Robbie left but she wasn't sure if he heard.

Beth leant against the motorbike and stared out of the cobwebbed window. She looked at her watch. She should be home from school by now. Would her mother have noticed? She'd been so upset with her last night. Beth didn't want that to happen again.

Slowly it dawned on her that she was gradually moving backwards. There was an almighty crash and she landed with a bump on something hard and incredibly sore – the motorbike.

Her foot was caught in the metal stand, and something else gashed deeply into her ankle.

'What did you do?' Robbie's red face appeared at the door. 'Everyone heard!'

Beth could take no more. She was cold, hungry and tired. 'I want to go home!'

Suddenly Robbie's mother's high anxious voice was

in the garden. 'Robbie, where are you? What happened? Is everything all right?'

'Hide,' Robbie whispered. Beth looked about but shelves full of paint, boxes of tools and a dark-green heavy-looking lawnmower provided no hiding place. The door opened and Robbie's plump mother stood in the frame. She stared at the bike on the ground and gasped. 'Jack's bike. Robbie how could you?' Next she stared at Beth, her pyjama bottoms and large black jacket. 'Who?'

'I'm –'

'She's nobody,' Robbie interrupted. Grabbing Beth's hand, he pulled her out of the shed, across the garden and into the kitchen.

Dorothea stood in the kitchen, her mouth hanging open. 'Robbie?'

Ignoring her, Robbie ran to the crack in the wall, and rubbed it with his free hand. Immediately the sucking sensation began and Beth knew she was going home. This time she relaxed into it and found the pressure less intensive. Within moments she and Robbie were spat onto her bed.

He pushed her off. 'You broke the brake levers on Jack's Matchless 350 ex-works. He's going to go into orbit.'

Beth rubbed her leg. 'Look at my ankle.'

'That bike cost one hundred pounds.'

'That's not very much.'

'Shut up!' Robbie was very red in the face. In fact Beth had never seen him so scarlet. He was marching about her room, arms going up and down like pistons.

'Stop making so much noise. My brother will hear you.' She pulled a warm hooded sweatshirt over her head and thick socks onto her frozen bare feet. Suddenly there was a thump followed by a squeal and Robbie's mother lay sprawled on Beth's bed.

'Mum?' Robbie gazed in horror. 'What are you doing here?'

'Where am I?' His mother looked around in a daze. Immediately her hand moved to check that her curls were still in place.

'You're in my room.' Robbie's mother smelled strongly of lavender, which made Beth sneeze. 'Ati-shoo!'

'Your room?' Robbie's mother looked at Beth first and then around. 'I don't understand.'

'It's alright Mum, there's nothing to understand. We'll go home now.'

'Home?' She sat up and reorganised her skirt. 'But I was at home. I didn't go anywhere.'

'You did,' Beth explained. 'You went through the wa–'

'Don't listen to her,' Robbie interrupted. 'Come on, Mum, we'll go.' He stepped onto the bed. But before Robbie could reach out to rub the crack, Jack and Dorothea came bursting through the wall, flattening both Robbie and his mother beneath them.

'Oh, my goodness! Jack, Dorothea, what on earth is going on?' Robbie's mother whimpered. 'Please move!'

'I saw you.' Dorothea wriggled out from under the

pile of limbs, 'and her, disappearing into the kitchen wall.' She hiccupped.

'Robbie. What have you done this time?' Jack looked about grimly, his usually perfect hair quite ruffled.

'It was her.' Robbie pointed at Beth.

Beth's chest puffed out with indignation. 'You started it!'

'Oh, for God's sake!' Jack disentangled himself from his mother and fell off the bed.

Dorothea stood beside him shivering. 'I feel funny.'

'It'll wear off,' Robbie said gruffly.

'What will wear off? What was that?' Jack looked back at the wall, as if it might hold some clues. 'Oh.' He spotted Beth for the first time. 'You're the English girl.'

'I'm Irish actually...' Beth tailed off, sick of explaining her family history.

Isabelle scrambled to her feet, pulling her blouse straight and checking her hair once more. She gave Beth a polite smile, 'Well, it was very nice to see your, eh, room but I think it's time that we all went home now.'

'Yeah, good idea.' Robbie moved towards the wall.

'Wait a minute.' Jack put out a hand. 'You say this is your house.' He peered out of the window overlooking the back garden. 'How can we be downstairs in our kitchen one minute and upstairs in your bedroom the next?' He turned to face her.

Beth opened her mouth but nothing came out.

'There's got to be some explanation for this.'

'Yes.' Robbie's mother nodded. 'You can't just tumble into one house from another. I felt as if my limbs were being pulled off.' She tittered nervously still patting her hair.

'And my ears.' Jack rubbed his rather large ones.

'I don't know.' Beth shrugged.

Robbie's mother gazed around baffled. 'It's the strangest thing.'

Dorothea studied Beth's bookshelf. 'I've never seen any of them before. What's Harry Potter about?'

'A boy who goes to wizard school.'

'Gosh!' Dorothea's eyes were huge. Next she picked up a fancy pink pen with a feather sticking out the top of it. 'What's this?'

'A pen. You can have it if you want.'

'Thank you!' Dorothea clasped it in delight. 'Smashing!'

'Look, what else she's got,' Robbie said pulling open the drawer at Beth's desk. 'A stapler, white stuff that crosses out mistakes, and, you're not going to believe this – her own phone.'

'No!' Dorothea gasped at the pink object.

'Don't be silly, Robbie.' His mother laughed nervously. 'That's impossible.'

'Yee har!' Robbie twirled in circles on Beth's office chair.

'Give me a go,' Dorothea squealed so Robbie put her on his knee and spun her in circles with him.

'Stop it, you'll make her sick.' Jack admonished but then smiled at Beth, a very charming smile. 'Might your sister be about?'

'Maybe,' she said slowly.

'Might I say hello?'

'Oh, yes.' Robbie's mother turned to her. 'We must meet your family. I feel terribly awkward arriving uninvited like this.'

'Eh…okay.' Beth led them out onto the landing

'Oh!' Robbie's mother exclaimed. 'This is rather like our house, don't you think?'

'Yes,' Jack frowned. 'Except that door shouldn't be over there.' He pointed at Beth's mother's and father's room.

'Oh, that's the extension.' Beth explained. 'We built it on when we moved in.' She led them down the stairs. 'I'll just pop my head into the kitchen and see who's there.'

'If your mother is busy, tell her we'll wait in the front room,' Isabelle said.

Beth hid a smile. 'Oh, she won't be.' Sure enough her mother was sitting on the sofa, staring at the wall with a deep crease between her brows. Jessica was at the stove stirring a pot of something. Cormac was glaring at a piece of music lying open on the kitchen table.

Jess saw Beth and waved her hand in a frantic come-over gesture. 'You've been ages.'

'Couldn't help it.'

Sylvie turned her head. 'What's going on?'

'Eh, we have some visitors.'

'Oh?' Sylvie's brows rose. 'Who?'

'A boy I know, his mother, brother and sister.'

'His brother?' Jess squealed.

'Don't shriek, Jessica.'

'They're just outside.'

'Oh!' Sylvie looked surprised. 'I'm glad you're making friends, darling, but today really isn't the best time—'

'Wait!' Jessica dumped the wooden spoon she was holding and hastily tugged at her ponytail so that it arched off the top of her head like a fountain. 'Okay.' She smoothed down her top.

Beth went to the door and pulled it open.

Jack walked in first. 'Hello again!' he said looking directly at Jessica.

'Hi!' Jessica grinned.

'I'm pleased to meet you.' Jack held out his hand to Sylvie. 'My name is Jack and this is my mother, Isabelle.' Jack opened his arm to allow his mother walk forward.

'I'm terribly sorry.' Robbie's mother patted her curls. 'I've no idea how we arrived here like this but I'm delighted to make your acquaintance.' She gave a nervous laugh.

Sylvie's smile broadened. 'I hope Beth hasn't been telling you I'm famous,' she tinkled.

'No way!' Beth flushed furiously.

Next Robbie walked in leading a scared-looking Dorothea. 'This is Dorothea.'

'Hello.' Sylvie sat up very straight. She had been a ballerina before she was an actress and her posture was perfect. 'Do you live close by?'

Robbie grinned. 'Very close by.'

Isabelle rushed to the windows. 'Oh how lovely – to have windows all the way along the wall like this.' She peered out at the rain battering down.

'Yes,' Sylvie agreed. 'There was a pokey old kitchen here when we moved in. The size of a cupboard really. And we wanted to take advantage of the south-facing garden so we knocked down the outer wall and built this.'

'How extraordinary,' Isabelle said frowning. 'Your back wall is exactly like ours.'

'Well,' Sylvie said. 'I presume it's the same estate.'

'I see,' Isabelle said looking as if she didn't see at all.

'Hey, what's this?' Jack peered in the round window of the washing machine.

'Whirlpool, I think,' said Sylvie.

'Is it for washing clothes?'

Sylvie snorted. 'Of course it is.'

Isabelle broke out of her daze by the window. 'What did you say about clothes?'

Jack tugged open the door. 'Look Mum, you put

them in there.'

Isabelle peeked inside. 'And then what happens?'

Sylvie mouthed to Beth behind their backs, 'Who are these people?'

'The machine tumbles them around in circles,' Jack said delighted.

Robbie's mother stared in wonder. 'Oh my goodness.'

'Would anyone like a cup of tea?' Jessica interrupted.

'Oh, that would be lovely, dear.' Robbie's mother straightened up.

'Let me help.' Jack strode across to Jessica and began joking quietly with her as they pulled mugs out of the cupboard. Beth watched him with narrow eyes.

Robbie's mother sat down beside Sylvie. 'You've a lovely home.'

'Thank you.' Sylvie tucked her bare feet under her bottom. 'But I'm afraid things are a bit all over the place at the moment, you see—'

Isabelle interrupted, 'Oh, I understand completely.

I'm so sorry to be arriving at such an hour. Five o'clock is a terrible time to have visitors, so close to dinner, I mean.' Isabelle looked around the empty kitchen. 'You must be very busy. I'm lucky I have Mary. She's making a pot roast this evening.'

'Is she your daughter?'

'Oh, no, our maid.'

Sylvie's eyebrows rose. 'Lucky you!'

'Don't you have anyone to help?' Isabelle's eyes widened.

'Goodness no! I do everything myself.'

Beth and Jessica glanced at one another in disbelief.

'Here we are.' Jack arrived with a tray of steaming mugs.

Robbie's mother stared at the tray with a puzzled expression. 'Saucers?'

'Eh…they don't seem to have any.' Jack looked embarrassed.

'Never mind!' Isabelle gave a false cheery laugh. Jack handed her a mug of tea and she frowned at the sight of a tea bag floating at the top. 'Oh, what's that?'

'I left the bags in,' Jessica explained stepping forward. 'I didn't know how strong you'd want it.'

'Oh,' Isabelle said faintly.

'Want to come upstairs?' Beth heard Jessica murmur quietly to Jack.

Suddenly Robbie's mother coughed and spluttered until tea ran out of her nose. Beth couldn't help laughing and Robbie openly snorted.

'Here.' Jack whipped a handkerchief out of the breast pocket and handed it to her.

'Oh my goodness!' She moped her eyes. 'Thank you darling.'

'Coming?' Jessica stood waiting at the door.

Jack quickly followed.

'Well, that's very forward, don't you think? How old is your daughter?' Isabelle gazed after them with an open mouth.

'Fifteen,' Sylvie said with pride.

'Well, really!'

'I know,' Sylvie laughed. 'She's so confident.' Then glancing at Beth. 'She makes poor little Beth seem the mouse of the family. My mother died six months ago, and since then,' she reached out to run her hand over Beth's hair, 'she's become quieter still. It's that difficult age, I suppose.'

'Oh!' Isabelle sighed. 'Robbie has been dreadful too. Ever since… well, ever since I can remember, actually.'

Sylvie looked over at Robbie. 'I can see that.' She smiled at his sour expression. 'I gave my mother a dreadful time too.'

'You didn't!' Isabelle gazed at her.

'Oh yes. I used to flit around doing what I liked. She never used to know where I was, but she was always wonderfully patient. And when I had the children, well,' Sylvie's eyes filled with tears, 'Mum was my rock…'

'Oh, you poor darling!' Isabelle put a hand on Sylvie's arm.

Sylvie gulped back tears, 'I'm sorry.'

Robbie's mother jumped up. 'No, *I'm* so sorry for intruding. I don't really know how it happened. My husband will be wondering what's happened to us. We'd better be going. Thank you so much.'

'Goodbye.' Sylvie attempted a smile. 'It was nice to meet you.'

'Robbie, Dorothea!' Isabelle called in a shrill voice marching into the hall. 'Jack! Downstairs please!'

'That isn't how you go home,' Beth said by the front door.

Isabelle frowned. 'Don't be silly, dear. Now, are you going to open the door for us?'

Beth opened the front door, and everyone took a step backwards. The rain was heavier now. It bounced and splashed off the driveway. The dark green bushes at the wall shook under the weight of it. A sudden rush of cold wind swept into the hall, splashing their faces with raindrops. 'Really!' Robbie's mother exclaimed. 'This weather wasn't forecast.'

She stepped outside but the moment her foot

landed on the pavement there was an almighty bang. 'What was that?' She stumbled backwards.

'Thunder!' Robbie said with delight. 'And here comes the lightning!' He pointed at the sky, which lit up like a television screen.

'Oh my!' They all stared in wonder at a jagged fork of light streaking overhead.

'Get down!' Robbie's mother grabbed the three children to her ample bosom.

There was a loud crack and the walls of the house shuddered like jelly on a plate. Then came the sound of tumbling bricks from inside. 'We've been hit!' Isabelle whimpered.

Sylvie came dashing into the hall. 'What was that?'

'Lightning,' Jack said hurrying down the stairs. He pushed opened the door to the front room. 'Look!'

Robbie followed Jack, after him came Sylvie, Isabelle, Beth and trailing behind Jessica and Dorothea.

'It's collapsed.' Jack pointed at the fireplace.

Sylvie coughed, waving away the dust. 'What a

mess! We're going to have to get the roof fixed, rebuild the chimney and re-plaster this room.' She squinted through the dust at bricks and plaster on the floor.

Isabelle stepped forward. 'I'm terribly sorry about your troubles but I don't suppose you have an umbrella?' she politely inquired.

'What?' Sylvie turned around.

'Well, we were just on our way...'

'Oh, yes.' Sylvie muttered. 'Jessica, go find one.'

'You don't need an umbrella,' Robbie said tugging his mother back into the hall.

'Of course we do. We'll be drenched!' The rain increased its downfall to emphasise her point.

'But Mum,' Robbie urged, 'don't you remember how we got here?'

His mother looked dazed. 'Not really.'

'You've got to go back upstairs to my room.' Beth put a foot on the stairs. 'Come on.'

'But—' Robbie's mother glanced at the front door.

'We'll show you.' Robbie shoved her in the direction

of the stairs. She continued looking over her shoulder as they pushed and pulled her up to the landing.

Beth opened the door to her room, took a step inside and let out a scream.

'What?' Robbie rushed in behind her, and like Beth, stared open-mouthed. Crumbled lumps of plaster-board, and broken bricks were all over Beth's bed and the floor beside it.

'Oh no!' Beth wailed.

Robbie rushed over to the bed and felt the exposed crumbling bricks. Nothing happened. 'The crack's gone.'

Beth pushed him aside to look. 'What are we going to do?'

'Your poor mother will have to get this wall fixed as well as the one downstairs.' Isabelle sighed. 'Well. I'm sorry to leave her like this, really I am, but Ron will be wondering where we are.'

Beth looked at Robbie, and Robbie looked at Beth. Neither of them wanted to be the one to say that now the wall was in smithereens, they had no idea how to transport his family home.

'Come on, Robbie.' His mother bustled onto the landing.

'We can't.' Robbie squeaked. 'We don't know how to get back.'

'Don't be silly!'

'It's true.' Beth faced her. 'We used to go through the wall.' She pointed at the crumbling wall. 'Here.'

'Through a wall?' Robbie's mother gave a hysterical laugh. 'Now stop it. I've had enough for one day. I'm tired.'

Robbie raised a brow at Beth. Now what?

Beth had no idea. What on earth were they going to do with Robbie, his mother, Dorothea and Jack stuck in their house with no way of getting them home?

CHAPTER FOURTEEN

'I thought you'd gone.' Sylvie frowned when everyone trooped into the kitchen once again.

'Yes, I'm sorry but your daughter and my son are behaving most peculiarly and not allowing me to go home.'

'We can't!' Robbie said, exasperated.

'Stop being so ridiculous. I'm going through that front door this instant. I've a pie to go into the oven, a pot of potatoes to boil, and a head of lettuce to wash. Your father will have nothing to eat!' she said almost in tears as she dashed into the hall.

'Our house isn't out there!' Robbie called after her.

'Give it up, Robbie,' Jack said tousling Robbie's hair. 'I don't know what you're playing at but it's time to stop.' He turned to Sylvie. 'I'm so sorry about your house. Is there anything I can do to help?'

Sylvie put a hand over her mouth and shook her

head. Jack said, 'Sorry,' once more awkwardly and followed his mother out of the front door. Beth and Robbie found them standing at the gate, staring into the street. 'This doesn't make sense,' Isabelle said faintly.

Jack followed her index finger, which was pointing at a BMW three series. 'Gosh,' he said excited. 'I've never seen anything like it.'

'What's that?' she asked as a Range Rover drove past their gaping faces. 'It's enormous!'

'What's going on?' Jack turned on Robbie.

'I've been trying to tell you,' Robbie said crossly.

'It's still Hawthorn Road,' Beth stepped forward, 'but a little later.'

'What do you mean?' Jack took a handkerchief out of his top pocket and dabbed his upper lip.

Beth shrugged. 'You see, we're over sixty years ahead of you.'

'Yes, and I'm going to win the Isle of Man, TT this year.' Jack tucked his handkerchief back into his pocket and smiled.

'I know what it is,' his mother turned around excitedly. 'An American film set!'

'No, Mum,' Robbie said patiently. 'It's the twenty-first century.'

'Twenty-what?'

'The year two thousand and nineteen,' Beth explained.

'Don't be absurd. If it were two thousand and nineteen, as you call it, I'd be dead and Robbie here would be an old man.'

'Oh yeah!' Beth gazed at Robbie in amazement. 'You're right.'

'Come on, Dorothea, dear.' Isabelle put out her hand and stepped onto the path. 'This is our street. All we have to do is find our house.'

Beth, Robbie, Jack and Jessica watched her and Dorothea walk down the street peering into each house and jumping in from the road every time a car drove passed.

'They're going terribly fast,' Jack said leaning out into the street to get a better look.

'They can go over one hundred miles per hour,' Robbie said.

'Don't Robbie.' Jack put a hand on the wall. 'I feel strange.'

The skin on his cheeks had gone pale green. Beth felt sorry for him. 'Come inside.'

Jess appeared on the stairs when they entered the hall. 'Do you want to come up to my room?'

'No.' Jack stumbled into the front room. 'I need to sit down.'

Jess and Beth followed him in. Jack sat on the low sofa, looking a darker shade of green. 'I can't believe this is happening.' He looked up. 'It's true?'

'Yeah.' Jess took his hand. 'I know it's weird.'

Jack shook away her words like rain. 'Are you out of your mind?' He stood up. 'You're telling me we're years ahead in the future?' He turned around slowly. 'So that's why you speak so strangely.'

Jess smiled. 'Me? You say spiffing, fagged out, and smashing.'

'Does no one say smashing anymore?'

'Not even my Dad.'

Jack sank back down. 'So this is where Robbie has been disappearing to?'

'Almost every afternoon,' Beth ventured.

'I don't feel well.' Jack put a hand over his mouth.

'Quick.' Jess pulled him into the hall, opened a door under the stairs and shoved him inside. From outside the door Beth and Jess heard Jack hurling the contents of his stomach into the toilet.

'Are you all right?' Jess called in anxiously.

Jack retched again.

Moments later, Robbie's mother returned into the house, her face grey and the pupils of her eyes huge. 'I don't like it here,' she panted. 'I'm frightened.'

At this Dorothea began to cry.

'Oh dear.' Robbie sighed and put his arm around his sister.

'Why don't you come back to the kitchen?' Beth said kindly.

'Yes, thank you.'

At that moment Jack emerged from the downstairs toilet.

'Jack.' Isabelle reached out to him.

'It's alright Mum.' He took her upper arms. 'We'll sort this out.'

'Jack to the rescue,' Robbie said under his breath.

'What was that?' Jack whipped around.

'Nothing,' Robbie said with a saccharine smile.

'If you've nothing useful to contribute, belt up!'

'I've been trying to tell you all along but you wouldn't listen.'

'When can you ever be trusted?'

'Oh leave me alone.' Robbie scowled, pulling his sobbing sister into the kitchen.

'Still here?' Sylvie asked puzzled when they all entered.

Robbie settled Dorothea at the table before answering. 'We can't go home, we're stuck here.'

'What do mean stuck?' Sylvie queried. 'People don't get stuck.'

'Yes they do.'

'Well get un-stuck. I'm sorry if this comes across as rude but…' She glanced out of the window. 'If the rain's a problem, I can drive you.'

'Do you drive a motor car?' Isabelle had overheard from the hall.

'Of course I do.' Sylvie snapped. 'Now tell me where you live and we'll go.'

'3 Hawthorn Road,' Isabelle murmured.

'3 Hawthorn Road? Is that a joke?'

Beth shook her head. 'No, Mum.'

'You can't live in Number 3 Hawthorn, that's our house.'

'It's ours too,' Jack said looking serious.

'You must mean 3 Hawthorn Terrace.'

'No,' Isabelle said shaking. 'It's road. I know it is. Ron has it on our headed paper.'

Sylvie laughed. 'Jess, what number is our house?'

'3,' Jessica said quietly.

'Can someone please tell me what the hell is going on?'

'You'd better sit down.' Beth led Sylvie to the sofa and sat down beside her. 'Robbie and his family used to live here.'

'You mean, before us?'

Beth and Jess exchanged glances. 'Quite a bit before us.'

'Oh, I see.' Sylvie relaxed. 'Well, why didn't someone tell me?' She turned to Isabelle. 'What are you doing back here?'

'I don't know.' Isabelle mopped a stray tear away with a linen handkerchief pulled from her sleeve. 'I was adding a little bit of porridge to the top of my crumble to make it crunchy, the way Ron likes it, when I heard a crash coming from the shed. I found Robbie there with your daughter Beth. They'd knocked over Jack's motorbike and when I was cross with Robbie he ran. They dashed in the back door. One minute they were in the kitchen and next they were gone. They literally disappeared into the wall before my very eyes. I reached my hand out and next thing I knew I was here.'

'You went through the wall.' Dorothea hiccupped. 'I saw you.'

'What wall?' Sylvie asked.

'In the kitchen.' Jack stepped forward. 'Dorothea showed me how to rub it, along a crack. I didn't believe her, of course, but she made me try it and that's how we ended up in your house.'

Sylvie shook her head. 'I've heard a lot of unbelievable stories in my time, but that takes the biscuit. Through a wall!'

'I don't understand it either.' Jack looked at Jess. 'May I have a glass of water?'

'Of course.' She hurried to the sink.

'So,' Sylvie said, 'you're telling me you used to live in this house and today you somehow landed up here again?'

'Yes.' Jack nodded while drinking.

Isabelle paced the room. 'Whatever will Ron be thinking? In all our years of marriage, he's never returned home to find no dinner.'

'Oh for goodness sake!' Sylvie snapped. 'Is he an invalid?'

'An invalid?' Isabelle asked dazed.

'Listen to me.' Sylvie's tone changed. 'If you're some kind of con-artists, trying to lay claim to this house, you don't have a chance. I've got the full deeds. Every court in the country will be on our side.'

'Mum,' Beth urged. 'That's not it.'

'We don't own the house,' Jack added. 'We're tenants.'

'Ron's saving.' Isabelle explained. 'He won't buy until he's ready. He's a banker you see.'

Sylvie sighed. 'No, I don't see.' The two women stared at one another. Neither of them had anything more to say.

* * *

As it happened, Ron Montgomery was wondering where his wife and family had gone. He'd arrived home at 6.20 p.m. as per usual and called out into the hall. 'Hello Darling!' but heard nothing in reply. Now this was unusual but not startling, it probably meant that Isabelle was collecting the washing in the garden, Robbie was out causing trouble – hopefully far away – Dorothea was reading in her room and Jack was tinkering with his bike in the garage. So, telling himself he'd find his wife and family soon, Ron placed his hat on the wooden hook in the hall, hung his coat below it, wiped his feet several times on the mat inside the door – Isabelle became cross if he forgot to – and smoothed down his hair whilst looking in the hall mirror. It was then that another anomaly struck him, one that he could simply not ignore – there was no whiff of roast chicken, no savoury aroma of soup on the stove or heavy smell of salty bacon. Perhaps Isabelle had a slice of fish for supper to put on the pan at the last minute. She liked to keep his fish fresh until he was settled at the table and she was sure it wouldn't be spoiled. That must be it he thought comforted, but then what about the soft starchy steam of potatoes? Shouldn't he at least smell those? Isabelle always boiled potatoes with fish. While this stream of thoughts flashed through his mind, he ambled along the hall to the kitchen door.

Inside the domestic centre of their home, the scene was even more disturbing: the table was cluttered with evidence of preparation for cooking but no finished article. There was raw flour sprinkled on one section, apple cores and skins, used utensils collected together, peeled potatoes – their skins still beside them – and a Pyrex dish holding a chicken and broccoli pie, at least that's what he thought it was. But instead of golden crusty pastry, the lid was pale, uncooked and still glistening, wet with egg yolk. 'Isabelle?' Ron's voice wavered.

In answer the back door burst open. 'Oh, Sir. I can't tell you what's happened!' Mary rushed in and burst into tears.

'Calm yourself, Mary, please!' Ron said, feeling any-thing but calm himself. 'Tell me what happened.'

'I don't know!' she wailed.

'Where are Isabelle and the children?'

'It wasn't my fault!' She clutched at him desperately.

'Of course it wasn't. Now sit down and tell me.' He waited for her to settle and then she began to speak.

'I'd only popped down to McCormack's to buy milk for the custard, we should have ordered more this week on account of all the extra baking we've been doing but we forgot.'

'Go on.'

'Well, when I got back to the house.' She searched his eyes. 'They'd gone.'

'All of them?'

She nodded.

'Jack, too?'

'I don't know. He wasn't back from work when I left.'

'Is he in the house now?'

'No.' She inhaled in a jerky shudder. 'I've searched high and low. None of them are anywhere.'

'There must be an explanation for this.' Ron barked a short laugh, the type of nervous noise he made when dealing with wills of particularly difficult clients. 'I mean families don't just disappear.'

'No, sir.' Mary stared at him.

'Perhaps Isabelle was called out to an emergency. Robbie probably got himself into some sort of trou-ble.'

'Yes Sir.' Mary nodded eagerly. 'I hadn't thought of that.'

'Well, let's just pop out to the neighbours. They might have seen them.'

'Right ho.' Mary wiped her eyes with her apron. She was about to blow her nose in it too, but thought better of it.

'I'll take the Murphys and the Becketts on the left, you go into Mrs Booth and the Moran's on the right.'

Fifteen minutes later each returned searching the other's face for news.

'Nothing.' Mary began to sob again. 'No one knows anything.'

'The Hall's heard a crash in the back garden then Isabelle calling Robbie's name.'

'That might mean something.' Mary clutched at his arm.

'We might check the garden once more.' He gently removed her hand and led her around the side of the house where, of course, they found nothing but Jack's bike lying awkwardly in the shed. Ron tut-tutted. 'Robbie just can't keep his hands off it.'

'You don't think Jack did something to him, do you?' Mary gazed with worried eyes.

'No.' Ron chuckled. 'Much more likely that Robbie found some further trouble and Isabelle, Jack and Dorothea followed in an effort to get him out of it.'

CHAPTER FIFTEEN

Beth and Robbie burst into the kitchen with very red faces. 'We've rubbed every crack in every wall but nothing works.'

'Stop.' Sylvie put a hand on her forehead. 'Just stop this.'

Isabelle gazed with longing at the comfortable sofa. 'Would it be possible to sit down?'

'Of course.' Sylvie shifted sideways.

'Thank you.' Isabelle sank back into the cushions. 'I have to say this is the oddest day of my life.'

'You're not the only one.'

Isabelle faced her. 'Yes, it must be awfully awkward for you. Is your husband due home?'

Sylvie clasped her hands together. 'No. I'm afraid my husband is in hospital.'

'Oh, I'm sorry. I hope it's not serious.'

'Well, not really… it's pneumonia.'

'Pneumonia!' Isabelle gasped. 'Oh, you poor dear.'

'The doctors say he'll be fine.'

'But pneumonia,' Isabelle repeated. 'That's not to be trifled with. What are you going to do without him?'

'Muddle through, I suppose. He will get better… but he won't be able to work for months and he's self-employed so that means no income, and I'm paid a pittance at the theatre.'

Isabelle's eyes opened wide. 'Theatre?'

'Yes,' Sylvie gave a brief a smile. 'I'm an actress.'

'Oh, how daring!' Isabelle whispered. 'I've never met an actress before.' Isabelle's body quivered with excitement. 'Are you acting in something at the moment?'

'Yes,' Sylvie sighed, 'but I couldn't care less about it, now. It's stupid anyway. The audience will never believe I'm Jane Austen's Emma. I should be playing her governess, but I kicked up a fuss and the director gave me the part.' Sylvie fiddled with the bangles on her wrist. 'But at least the money will come in handy. Not that theatre pays very much.'

'They pay you?'

'Of course! But television pays better. For years my acting supported us all while Bill attended veterinary college.'

'Oh my goodness!' Isabelle gazed at her in wonder.

* * *

Robbie and Beth left their mothers sitting side by side and slipped into the sitting room, which was mercifully empty. Beth sat down and Robbie paced the room with hands in his pockets.

'Is the kitchen the only place you could get to our house from your house?' Beth questioned.

'Yes,' Robbie said. 'I never came any other way.'

'Did you visit the people who lived here before us too?'

'No.' He faced her. 'I only started at the beginning of September.'

'Why?'

'The crack wasn't in the kitchen wall before then.'

'Oh. I wonder what caused it.'

Robbie shrugged.

'What made you rub your hand along it?'

'I was trying to peel off the plaster.'

'Why?' Beth paused and shook her head. 'Actually, it doesn't matter.'

'I'd only been coming here a couple of days before you found out.'

Beth sat back into the chair. 'I wonder what caused the cracks.' There wasn't one in her room when they first moved in. 'Do you think it could have been the extension?'

'When was that?'

'August.'

Beth and Robbie stared at each other. 'Maybe,' Robbie sat down beside her. 'The builders must have knocked down the original back wall of our house to make that huge room at the back. And they also knocked down our old kitchen wall so that it could join up with that big room.'

'Yeah.' Beth nodded. 'But why did it cause a crack

in my room?'

Robbie jumped up. 'It's the same wall that was in our kitchen. '

'The same wall?'

'Yes, it used to run along the centre of the house upstairs and downstairs. So the wall in your room is the same wall that used to be in our kitchen, before you knocked it down.'

'And us knocking it down caused a crack in it sixty years earlier?'

'Yes and a crack in your room now.'

'It doesn't make any sense.' Beth looked glum. 'If only I hadn't followed you back–'

Robbie shook his head. 'I'm glad did. You were doing me a favour. No one's ever tried to help me before. You're the only person who doesn't think I'm stupid.'

'You're absolutely not!'

'My parents think I am.'

Beth bit her lip. 'I guess you breaking things doesn't help.'

Robbie blew his fringe out of his eyes. 'Why does no one understand that I'm trying to figure out how they work?'

'I get it,' Beth said softly. 'And I'm glad you slipped through the walls too.'

'Are you?' Robbie looked surprised.

'Yeah. I hated everything here before you came along.'

'Why?'

'I wanted to be back in London. My best friend's there, and that's where Gran lived.'

'Where's she now?'

It was Beth's turn to study the floor. 'She died.'

'Oh,' Robbie slid along the sofa beside Beth.,'I'm sorry.'

'Thanks,' she said. He was almost twice the size of her, but having him beside her felt warm and comforting.

'We're just going to have to muddle through this.' Robbie rubbed his forehead.

'Your mum doesn't seem to get that we're stuck here.'

Robbie sighed. 'I don't think she wants to.'

Suddenly Isabelle bustled into the room, confused and baffled. 'I don't know what's happening.'

Robbie stood up and put an arm around her. 'We're stuck in the future, mother.'

'Stop it. I don't like you talking like that. If you insist we can't go home, I must make a meal. It's almost six o'clock. You must be starving, poor things!'

Robbie rubbed his stomach. 'I'm certainly hungry.'

'I don't like to disturb your mother,' Isabelle said to Beth. 'She seems to have fallen asleep on the sofa. Perhaps you, Dorothea and I could prepare the evening meal. Maybe if you tell me what your mother has planned...'

Beth looked puzzled. 'Well, eh, we might order take-away?'

'What?' Isabelle asked.

'An Italian or an Indian.'

'Is that some sort of meal?'

'Yes. I'll show you.' Beth led her into the kitchen, grabbed a bunch of colourful menus from behind the microwave and gave them to Isabelle. 'Anything there can be here in twenty minutes.'

Isabelle read the first leaflet. Bruschetta, Spaghetti Carbonara, pizza and calzone. She picked up the next leaflet. Chicken Masala, Naan bread, poppadums. She put the leaflets aside as if they were of no use. 'Well, everyone must be getting hungry, don't you think we should get started?' Isabelle rolled up her sleeves. 'I don't want to depend on your hospitality without doing my bit.' She looked about the large kitchen. 'May I have an apron?' Isabelle smoothed down her mauve woollen dress.

'There might be one of Gran's about the place.'

'That would be wonderful. Thank you.' While Beth rummaged through drawers, Isabelle turned to Dorothea. 'Enough moping at the table,' she said briskly, 'we're going to prepare a lovely meal.'

Dorothea stood up and awaited instructions.

'You might make some of your lovely pastry.'

'Don't bother,' Sylvie said, opening her yes. 'We can make sandwiches. Jessica is good at those.' She yawned and stretched her arms either side of her head.

'Sandwiches?' Isabelle held on to the side of the table. 'That's all you feed them?'

'We've some cold meats from the deli.'

'But what about dinner?' Isabelle's voice trembled. 'I don't understand. Do you Dorothea?'

Dorothea shook her head.

Sylvie sighed. 'Don't worry about it.'

But Isabelle couldn't relax. 'Do you keep hens?' she asked hopefully.

'Hens?' Sylvie said stunned.

'Out the back.'

'We don't have time for that sort of thing.' Sylvie picked up some papers off her lap. 'Now, I've got to ring my agent.' She swept out of the kitchen.

Still clad in her apron, Isabelle walked to the fridge and asked Beth. 'Do you mind if I take a peek?'

'No,' Beth muttered. It was like watching an anxious butterfly flitting about the kitchen.

Isabelle opened the fridge door and peered inside, her large bottom ballooning behind her. 'How extraordinary! It's colder than our pantry.' She took out two packets of cold cooked chicken, some tomatoes, a cucumber and a bag of washed salad. 'Why is it all different colours?'

'It's different types of lettuce.'

'It's not poisonous?'

'No.'

Isabelle looked doubtful and put it back in the fridge. She took out a glass jar of mayonnaise, opened it up, sniffed it and scooped out a dollop with a spoon. She licked the spoon and placed the jar on the counter. 'Very nice.' She walked about the kitchen. 'May I?' she asked, one hand on a cupboard handle. 'I know I'm being dreadfully nosey.'

'It's alright.' Beth didn't think her mother would mind.

'My goodness.' Isabelle came face to face with shelves of instant noodles, boxes of easy-cook rice, bags of dried pasta, jars of curry and tomato sauce cluttered together. 'I've never seen anything like it. Do you think we could use some of these?'

'Sure.' Beth shrugged.

'Now, Dorothea.' Isabelle returned to the table clutching jars. 'Have a look in the garden. See if you can find some carrots and potatoes.'

Dorothea returned moments later. 'There's nothing Mam. Only grass and bushes.'

Isabelle turned to Beth. 'No vegetable patch?'

'We usually have rice or pasta.' But Isabelle didn't seem to understand what Beth was talking about. She had no idea how to cook pasta or even what it was so Beth tumbled dried pasta into a large pot of boiling water and added some salt.

'We don't have to peel anything?'

'No.'

'How marvellous!'

In under twenty minutes both families sat down to plates of pasta mixed with ready-cooked chicken, tomato sauce from a jar and a salad. 'That must be fastest meal in history!' Isabelle laughed.

* * *

Beth insisted that Robbie's family stay the night, but where was everyone to sleep? After some thought, Sylvie assigned Robbie the floor in Cormac's room, Jess moved into Beth's room, Dorothea and her mother took Jess's double bed and Jack was given the sofa downstairs. Sylvie kept her own room to herself and retreated there with obvious relief.

A few days later, Bill was discharged from hospital. He arrived home weak and in need of rest. 'Oh, hello,' he said when he saw Robbie and his family in the kitchen, 'Are you in a production with my wife?'

'No, Bill,' said Sylvie. 'They're not actors. Well, at least I don't think they are.'

'We most certainly are not.' Isabelle sniffed.

Bill smiled uncertainly. 'So who are you then?'

'They're friends of mine.' Beth stepped forward and proceeded to introduce Robbie's family to her father.

'Very pleased to meet you,' Bill said politely, sinking back into a chair at the table and closing his eyes. Sylvie gave him a gentle nudge.

'Eh… is everything all right?' he asked.

Sylvie said exasperated. 'They're here to stay.'

'Your wife has been most terribly kind,' Isabelle gushed.

'Do you have no money, is that it?' Bill asked Isabelle kindly.

'I do actually.' She fumbled in a small purse in the pocket of her apron. 'Just for buying odds and ends.' She opened her palm to display a collection of large brown coins and smaller silver ones of varying sizes.

'What are they?' Beth peered at the coins.

'These large copper ones with the hens on the front are pennies, the silver one with the hare is a thru penny, the one with the ground hound is six pence, the one with the pig and her piglets is a shilling, and this one's a farthing.' She gave Beth a tiny copper coin with a bird flying on it.

'What's a farthing?'

'Quarter of penny.'

'Give me strength!' Sylvie sighed.

'You can't buy much with them, can you?' Bill continued to talk to Isabelle.

'Well,' she relaxed a little. 'With a thru penny bit I can buy a pint of milk and a loaf of bread costs me four pence.'

'Oh.' Bill suddenly sniffed the air appreciatively. 'What's cooking?'

'Isabelle made dinner,' Sylvie forced a smile. 'Again.'

'Lovely!' He beamed.

'Sit down everybody.' Isabelle bustled up and down the table dolloping large spoons of roast potatoes, cauliflower and white sauce and roast chicken onto each person's plate.

'This is delicious.' Bill tucked in enthusiastically. Everyone but Sylvie agreed.

'I'm so glad you like it.' Isabelle was transformed from the panicked woman they'd come to know to a relaxed, domestic beauty. 'I was saying to Sylvie that you really should keep chickens.'

'You know, that's a good idea,' Bill agreed.

'And a vegetable patch,' Isabelle added.

'Yes,' Bill said helping himself to more potatoes. 'The children could get involved. Don't you think?' He looked at Sylvie.

Sylvie snapped. 'I think we've enough going on right now.'

'I hope you don't think I'm interfering,' Isabelle flashed Sylvie a smile. 'I just want to thank you for your hospitality.'

'Not at all, this is brilliant!' Bill beamed around the table.

'Bill. We need to talk,' Sylvie said as soon as he'd cleaned his plate. 'Isabelle, could you give our family some time together please?'

'Of course!' Isabelle pushed herself up from the

table. 'Jack will take us all out for a nice walk, won't you?'

'Yes, Mum.' Jack stood up. 'Robbie, Dorothea. Let's go.' Robbie followed with a scowl.

As soon as Sylvie shut the door behind them, she turned to Bill. 'We have to tell you something.' Sylvie sat at the table and took her husband's hand. 'Beth says she's been travelling back in time to this house in the 1950s. She says these people used to live here then.'

Bill coughed and took a sip of water.

'I don't get it.' He looked inquiringly at Beth.

'It's true,' Beth mumbled.

'Either our daughter is gone mad, or something altogether terrible is happening.' Sylvie shuddered.

'It's not just me,' Beth protested. 'Cormac and Jess have been there too.'

'Really?' Bill sat up straighter.

'I know it's hard to believe,' Jess joined in, 'but we really did travel back in time.'

'But how?'

'Through the wall in Beth's room.'

'You're having me on!' Bill spluttered.

'Honest, Dad. It was the most amazing thing!' Cormac yelled. Beth glanced at him in surprise. Usually Cormac never got excited about anything but his music.

'I don't understand. How did you get through the walls?' Bill rested the side of his head in one hand.

'We were kind of got sucked, and then we ended up in Robbie's kitchen.'

'This doesn't make any sense!' Bill shook his head tiredly.

'I know!' Sylvie threw up her hands. 'I haven't wanted to worry you, Bill. Not while you were in hospital.'

'Dad, it's true!' Beth insisted. 'And when lightning struck the roof of the house, the plaster fell off my wall and the crack in my room disappeared. Now they can't travel back anymore.'

'You see! Our children have lost their minds!'

Bill thought for a moment. 'You know, Beth doesn't look as if she's lost her mind.'

'She doesn't,' Sylvie conceded.

'Neither do Cormac or Jess.'

Sylvie tilted her head to one side. 'True.'

'And they are dressed unusually.'

'Bill!' Her voice held a note of warning.

'And she does have that old fashioned money.'

'Anyone could have that,' Sylvie argued. 'There are props like that to be got all over Dublin.'

'But if they were professional actors, you'd recognise them, wouldn't you?'

'Well … yes.'

'Then.' Bill sank back in his chair. 'I think we should believe them.'

'Believe them?' Sylvie's voice rose.

'Until proven otherwise.' He nodded.

'And what do we do with them? They've been here nearly a week. It's hardly convenient, especially with you sick.'

He shrugged. 'I'll be alright. Perhaps we can learn from them?'

'Learn from her?' Sylvie snorted with derision. 'A woman from the 1950s? I don't think so!'

He took her hands. 'We can at least be kind.'

Sylvie sighed. 'If you're as soft with animals as you are with humans I don't know how you put any of them down.'

Bill chuckled. 'I don't when I can avoid it.'

'It's not going to be easy.' Sylvie sighed. 'Jess and Beth have to share a room and Cormac has that wild boy, Robbie, in his room. His mother has no control over him whatsoever.'

'He's just a boy,' Bill said good-naturedly.

He didn't say that two days later when Robbie had broken his computer, taken apart Sylvie's phone and electrocuted himself with the toaster.

'Why can't he just leave things alone?' Bill asked Beth exasperated.

'I think he wanted to see how they work.'

'But now they don't work,' Bill complained.

'Sorry Dad, but Isabelle keeps saying she'll replace anything he damages.'

'Tell her not to worry about it.' Bill sighed. 'With a purse full of pennies, shillings and a farthing she's hardly in a position to buy a new iPhone.' Her father trudged off to lie down.

CHAPTER SIXTEEN

Cormac couldn't understand Robbie, and Robbie couldn't understand Cormac.

'Do you not do anything else?' Robbie asked when Cormac had being studying music and playing the piano non-stop all day long.

'I've exams in December.' Cormac turned over in bed so that his back was to Robbie.

'But what about football?'

'I don't have time.'

Robbie lay staring at the ceiling. 'How old are you again?'

'Ten.'

'You look about eight.'

'Just shut up!' Cormac said fiercely.

'I only said–'

'I don't want to hear!'

Robbie twiddled with his fingers in the dark. All

the gadgets they had here: computers giving information on anything in the whole world. And those tiny carry-about phones. Imagine if he and his friends had them in school. There would be no need to throw paper notes. If he could just work out now how they were designed, when he went home he could invent one and become famous. No one would be able to call him stupid again. Robbie drifted off to sleep happily.

* * *

Across the landing, Beth squirmed uncomfortably in her bed. Jess's large feet were level with Beth's head, and Beth faced the wall to keep away from them. Beth wondered how Robbie was getting on with Cormac. Her brother had been very cross about having to share.

'What about my work?' he'd yelled.

'Robbie will only sleep there. He won't be there during the day, will you, Robbie?' Sylvie asked him.

'No.' Robbie said but Beth didn't believe him. Robbie did whatever he liked no matter what anyone said. She couldn't help admiring him. Beth had always done what she was told by her mother, her father, her teachers and even her grandmother. It had never entered her head not to. But since getting to know Robbie it struck her that a parent couldn't actually force you to wear a bicycle helmet all the way to school, unless they cycled there with you themselves. A teacher couldn't force you to do your homework. It was perfectly possible to say no and slam the book shut. But Beth had never wanted to. She liked doing her homework. However, the option not to was an intriguing thought. Getting to know Robbie taught her she had more freedom than she ever knew – if she had the guts to take it.

Workmen were coming the next day to repair the wall on the side of the house, and Beth worried about what would happen then? Would Robbie and his family be able to travel home or would they be stuck here forever?

* * *

In his own time zone, Ron lay awake tears spilling

out of his eyes. His whole family gone: his beloved Isabelle; anxious, pretty Dorothea; solid, intelligent Jack and the ragamuffin Robbie. Without them his life was empty. He hated his job, writing columns of figures. The only reason he did it was to pay the rent on this fine house, to buy food for his family and to treat Isabelle with a new frock or piece of jewellery, when he could afford it. Once again he turned in the bed. The police had asked him all sorts of questions that evening, insinuating that he might have hurt Isabelle causing her to run away. As if that were possible?

Oh Lord, bring my family home to me, he prayed.

He prayed the same prayer the next night, and the next night too. By the third night, Ron's prayer had changed – he was praying not to go to prison.

'Murder?' he gasped at the police. 'Why would I kill what I cherish most in this world?'

'It's quite often a spouse,' the policeman said gravely, 'in cases like these.'

'And does "the spouse" trawl the streets of the city

searching for his wife? Does he lie awake at night praying for her return?'

'I really don't know, sir.'

'That's obvious.' Ron was uncharacteristically rude.

'The maid said there had been a row recently.' The policeman avoided eye contact and flicked through pages of a small black notebook.

'Row?' Ron said puzzled.

'Last Thursday evening it was.'

Ron racked his brain. What had they been doing last Thursday? It seemed an eternity ago, when all they had to worry about was Robbie's exams. 'Oh that was nothing,' he muttered.

'We'd like to hear about it please.'

'Oh all right.' He sighed. 'My wife was anxious about our son, the younger one. He gets into trouble.'

'What kinds of trouble?'

'Setting fire to things, knocking people over on his bicycle, damaging property.' Ron sighed.

The policeman's brows rose as he scribbled in his

little book. 'Has he ever been arrested?'

'No. People have been very understanding, and I've compensated for any damage done.'

'And what exactly were you and your wife arguing about that night?'

'Robbie had ripped up the school uniform for his new boarding school and covered it with tar from the road works on our street.'

The policeman suppressed a grin. 'Sounds a bit of a handful.'

Ron pulled a large cotton handkerchief out of his jacked and rubbed his bald spot. 'I had a full head of hair before Robbie.'

'And your wife was upset?'

'Oh yes, poor Isabelle. She didn't see how we could afford another uniform, and suggested we not send Robbie away at all. Now usually I agree with everything my wife wishes, but that evening I insisted on having my way. Robbie was in too much trouble.'

'Thank you, sir.' The policeman closed his notebook

and took his leave. Ron remained alone by the piano. How could he ever sing another note without Isabelle to accompany him?

CHAPTER SEVENTEEN

That next day Beth asked her mother if Robbie could attend her school.

'I don't think so Beth. The teachers wouldn't like it.'

'We could say he's my cousin.'

They both looked at Robbie's thick auburn hair, freckled face and ruddy red cheeks. 'I don't think so,' said Sylvie.

'But what will he do if he stays here all day long… with you?'

Sylvie put her hands on her hips and frowned. 'Yes, perhaps, it would be a good idea for him to go.'

'Great!' Beth grinned. 'Come on!' She grabbed Robbie and dragged him outside to her bike.

At school, Gráinne and her crew stared at Robbie in awe. 'How old are you?'

'Twenty-seven,' he replied coolly.

The girls tittered, knocking against each other like

skittles, and Robbie smirked.

Miss Fitzpatrick wasn't quite so impressed with him or Sylvie's letter. 'It's very short notice.' Her brows squeezed together creating a deep vertical line between them.

'It's only for a couple of days,' Beth pleaded.

'All right.' She sighed, 'But I don't know where we'll fit him.'

'Beside me,' Beth said firmly.

At break time a clutch of girls surrounded them. 'Where do you go to school?' Tanya Armstrong asked.

'Sandford Park.'

'Ooooh! Stuck up snob!'

'Not the one in Dublin.' Beth gave Robbie a quick kick. 'He goes to a different one in Galway.'

'Yeah, and I'm rolling in it. My father has two cars and his own yacht.'

'Big deal.' Gráinne yawned.

'Yeah, we've three cars,' Rebecca said casually.

'Well, our whole family went to America last year,'

Robbie lied.

'All the way to America. OMG!' Gráinne sneered and her crew of girls tittered with her.

'Come on, Robbie,' Beth said pulling him away. His cheeks were dangerously red and his eyes glittering.

Robbie scowled at Gráinne and her girlfriends for the rest of the class. When Miss Fitzpatrick asked him a question, he put his hand behind an ear and pretended he was deaf.

'Oh,' Miss Fitzpatrick said highly embarrassed. 'Beth, you should have told me, your cousin was hard of hearing.'

'Er … sorry,' Beth murmured.

At break time Robbie grabbed Beth's arm. 'Do you know where that skinny girl lives?'

'Gráinne?' Beth asked nervously. 'No.'

'We're going to find out.'

Although it was the last thing Beth wanted to do, Robbie insisted that they follow Gráinne and her crew after school. 'If they turn around just pretend to be tying your shoe lace,' he instructed.

'Okay,' Beth felt slightly sick. Her favourite time of day was cycling home in the opposite direction to Gráinne and her friends.

'When we find out where she lives, she'll be sorry,' he said with menace.

As it turned out, Gráinne's father didn't own three cars at all, or if he did they were nowhere to be seen. After waiting outside the local take-away for a bag of chips, divided between four girls and three rough-looking boys, Gráinne separated from the group and walked the last bit home on her own.

'That's funny,' Beth said. 'I thought she lived in Ranelagh.'

But Gráinne was walking in the opposite direction to the pretty, leafy Dublin village. She turned into a side alley behind a row of large houses. They watched Gráinne pull a key out of her pencil case and open a padlock hanging off a large metal gate.

Robbie pushed Beth flat against the wall. 'Don't let

her see us.'

But Gráinne was too intent on fiddling with the rusty-looking lock to notice them. Eventually it opened and she stepped inside, clanging the metal door behind her.

'Leave your bike here,' Robbie ordered.

Beth wasn't keen to leave her precious bike in a deserted alleyway but as there was nobody about she hoped it would be all right for a few minutes. 'What are we doing?' she whispered.

'Following her.' Robbie ran down to the gate that Gráinne had entered, and dragged an oversized bin alongside the wall. He scrambled on top of it. 'Come on.' He held out a hand for Beth. Holding her breath, so that she wouldn't have to breathe in the rubbishy smell from the bin, she hauled herself onto it.

They stood side by side looking down at a concrete courtyard and a small, stone cottage with latticed wooden windows and a pretty front door.

'She can't live there!' Beth exclaimed. Gráinne

always said she lived in a mansion not a cottage.

'Bet she does.'

'But she's rolling in it,' Beth panted. Suddenly Robbie leapt across to the wall. 'What are you doing?'

'Going in.' Robbie heaved himself up on the wall.

'What if she sees you?'

'Who cares?'

'I'm not coming.'

Robbie looked at her with such a mixture of scorn and disappointment that Beth couldn't bear it. 'I mean, wait.' Beth jumped up and fell onto the wall beside him. 'Ouch!' She almost slid off again; it was covered with bits of glass set into the concrete.

'Don't put your hands down,' he barked.

That was easier said than done. Using her elbows, Beth pushed herself upright, tearing a hole in the arm of her jumper as she did. 'Oh no!' she groaned but Robbie had already jumped down to the concrete below and was creeping towards a window. Beth glanced back at the bin below her. Could she jump back onto it? But the thought of falling backwards on the laneway was even less appealing than meeting Gráinne O'Reilly on her home ground.

Robbie gestured with his hand for her to follow and Beth supposed she might as well. Normally she would attempt to lower herself from a high wall, but the glass prevented her from using her hands, so she had to scrunch her body down as low as she could and spring off from her feet. Flying through the air reminded her of jumping off rocks into the sea but instead of meeting the welcoming splash of water, she landed on hard pavement sending a shudder through her bones.

'She's in there,' Robbie said peering in the window. Beth rubbed her sore knees and stumbled over to join him.

After a moment, she saw Gráinne tucking a blanket around a young child. She was singing.

'That doesn't sound like Gráinne,' Beth muttered. Picking up the baby, Gráinne disappeared into another room. 'Now what'll we do?'

'Come on.' Robbie crept towards the door.

Beth reached out to grab the back of his jumper but he'd already pushed open the front door, which creaked loudly.

'Who's there?' Gráinne reappeared before them, the baby in her arms.

'I came to see your Dad's three cars,' Robbie said leaning against the side of the door.

Gráinne became paler than usual.

Robbie looked around. 'So where are they?'

'Not here,' she said quickly. 'This isn't my house.'

'So why do you have a key?'

'I'm babysitting.' She jiggled the baby.

A tired, thin-looking woman with lank hair appeared. 'Who's this?' she said sharply.

'Kids from school.' Gráinne was sullen.

'We came to see Gráinne's dad's cars,' Robbie said.

'Gráinne's dad?' The woman laughed, except it wasn't a happy laugh. It was more like a yelp. 'Gráinne's father died last year.'

'Oh, no!' Beth put a hand to her mouth.

'Shut up!' Gráinne swiftly dumped the baby in the woman's arms and pushed Robbie and Beth out of the house. 'Who the hell do you think you are? How dare you spy on me?' Beth saw the glitter of tears in Gráinne's eyes. 'Get lost!' She slammed the door in their faces.

Beth and Robbie were left standing alone in the small courtyard. Robbie tried the gate but it was locked. Oh no, Beth thought. How would they get out again? The wall was too high to climb. But Robbie was scrambling up onto a sidewall that led to the roof of the small house. 'We'll go over the top and out the front.'

'Okay.' Anything was better than climbing back over the glass wall.

Five minutes later they had clambered over the roof of Gráinne's house and into a long garden behind a tall old-fashioned house. The grass was over-grown and there were ancient apple trees with grey mould growing on the barks.

'Hurry!' Beth said, thinking of her bicycle in the lane-way.

They walked through the long grass and down concrete steps to a back door. Robbie pressed against it and it pushed open.

Inside was dark and smelled of car oil. Robbie sniffed appreciatively. 'Engines!'

'Forget it.' Beth tugged at him.

They tiptoed through the dark to a flight of stone steps. Robbie went up first, taking two steps at a time with his long legs. Beth shivered behind him imagining rats in corners and spiders hanging from the ceiling.

There was a door at the top of the stairs. Robbie pushed against it but it didn't budge.

'Try again!' Beth urged.

'Okay.' He shoved one shoulder against it. The sound of thick gloopy paint becoming unstuck, preceded the door flying open. Robbie fell instantly forwards and landed splat on a black and red diagonally tiled floor.

'What's that? Who's there?' An ancient man, who looked about one hundred years old, hobbled into the hall. His thin upper body was curved like a question mark and white hair grew in tufts about his ears. 'I'll have the law on you.' He waved his stick. 'Breaking and entering.'

'Please, sir,' Beth stepped forward. 'We aren't here to steal. We got lost and we're trying to get home.'

'What did you say?' He put a shaky hand behind a large ear.

'We're LOST!' Beth yelled. 'We want to go home!' Robbie was rubbing his shoulder and wincing in pain.

The old man stuck out his stick like a barrier. 'Names?'

'Eh … Beth and Robbie.'

'Robbie?' The man stumbled. 'Where do you live?'

'Hawthorn Road.' Beth and Robbie chorused.

'Did you say Hawthorn?' The man's legs buckled and Beth ran to aid him before he hit the floor. Robbie grabbed his other side and together they guided him to a velvet chair by the wall. 'Hawthorn,' he muttered to himself. 'Haven't heard that in a long time.'

Beth mouthed, 'Come on,' at Robbie. He nodded and the two of them gently edged away from the old man, skittered across the hall, pulled open the front door and spilled down the steps to the street below.

Soon they were sprinting down the street as fast as they could. Beth thought she heard a voice calling for them to come back, but she and Robbie kept running.

CHAPTER EIGHTEEN

Ron watched the boy and girl run away. The first year after his family disappeared, Ron thought he'd seen Robbie, Isabelle, Dorothea and Jack everywhere he went. He'd followed look-alikes for miles, knocked on doors to be greeted with strange faces and even stranger looks. Later the sightings dried up when he realised he couldn't know what his family looked like anymore. Robbie, Jack and Dorothea would be adults and his beloved Isabelle an old woman. It was impossible to imagine.

But today was like one of the original sightings, the boy looked exactly as Robbie had done the day he disappeared – tall and lanky, with a long floppy fringe. Robbie was even wearing the tweed jacket with the patches on the elbow that Isabelle had patiently replaced every time he ripped one off.

Leaving the front door open, Ron hobbled to the

green velvet chair and slowly eased himself down. It was decades since his family had disappeared. Decades of despair and loneliness. He had never considered remarrying. How could he? No woman would ever compare with Isabelle.

Since his one hundredth birthday, a few years previously, he had received two congratulatory letters from the president and had his photograph in the newspaper. Still his stubborn heart kept beating. What was it waiting for? Thump, thump, thump. He knocked himself weakly on the chest. It was all so pointless. All he had was an empty old house to rattle about in, and a tired-looking cleaning woman who glared at him when she thought he wasn't looking. She wasn't the ideal home help. However the day she came knocking on his door, a baby on one arm and an unhappy young girl beside her, he had felt sorry for her. It had been her idea to move into the 'mews' at the back of the garden. She said it was impossible to find anywhere to rent in Dublin and would he be interested in letting it to her. Ron said, he had been meaning to rent it out but hadn't got around to tidying it up. She insisted that she could do it herself and told how her husband had recently died with no warning. She needed to move out of their large family home, as they could no longer afford it. The tale went straight to Ron's heart. This woman knew what it was like to lose family with no warning. They were two of a kind.

* * *

Twenty minutes later, Robbie and Beth arrived home with Beth's bicycle, which luckily was still waiting for her exactly where she'd left it.

'Where on earth have you been?' Isabelle peered out of the front door as if a monster might be chasing them down the street.

'Just out,' Robbie said. 'It's fine, Mum.'

'No, it is not fine.' Isabelle twisted a handkerchief in her hands. 'Nothing's fine! I didn't know where you were and… your father.' She sobbed.

'Come on, Mum.' Jack led her back to the kitchen,

glaring over his shoulder at Robbie. 'Why don't you ever do what you're told?'

'Oh shut up, Mr Perfect!' Robbie stomped upstairs where he found Cormac frowning at a blank music sheet at the small desk in his room. 'What you doing now?' he asked.

'Writing a symphony for the Christmas concert,' Cormac snapped.

Robbie lifted the page up to the light. 'Using invisible ink?'

'No!' Cormac snatched the sheet back.

'No need to be so ratty.'

'Your mother has been wailing all afternoon.'

'She's always doing that.'

'You're a spoilt brat, you know that?'

'Look who's talking.' Robbie settled himself on a beanbag and reached for Cormac's iPod.

'Don't touch that!' Cormac grabbed it off him.

'I was only looking!'

'Yeah, and we all know what happens when you

look at something.' Cormac slipped the precious iPod into his pocket.

'I just want to find out how it works.'

'Buy a manual. You're not supposed to look inside them. That's for the scientists.'

'That's what I'm going to be.' Robbie linked his hands over his stomach. 'A scientist.'

'Yeah, right.'

'And you're going to be a penis.' Robbie sniggered. 'Oh sorry, I meant pianist!'

'Shut up!' Cormac slammed a hand on his desk. 'You're so annoying!'

'I'm annoying? You're the most irritating, snotty, wimpy boy I've ever met.'

'I am not!'

'You are so. Your mother fusses over you the whole time. Cormac, don't run! Take care, Cormac! Wrap up warm! Cormac, Cormac, Cormac!' Robbie imitated Sylvie's voice.

'Stop it!

'Beth already told me what you were like and she was right.'

Cormac's voice became almost a whisper. 'What did Beth say?'

'That you're a pain and really boring.'

Suddenly Cormac charged at Robbie. 'Get out of my room, get out of my house!' He kicked and slapped in a frenzy, shoving Robbie right out of the door onto the landing.

Just at that moment, Sylvie emerged from her room and saw Cormac's arms swinging wildly. 'Cormac! Stop it!'

But Cormac didn't appear to see his mother, let alone hear her; he was too busy venting all his rage and frustration on Robbie.

'Get off!' Sylvie grabbed Cormac and shoved him into his bedroom and slammed the door. 'Now,' she turned to Robbie, 'what was that all about?'

'I told your drippy son what I thought of him,' Robbie said.

'You did?' Sylvie put her hands on her hips. 'And do you still think he's a drip?'

Robbie rubbed his face. 'He's more spunk than I thought.'

'You all right?'

Robbie checked a few body parts. 'Nothing broken.'

'Good. Now, I'll get Cormac to apologise.'

Robbie sighed. Why did adults always have to go and mess things up just when a situation had been sorted?

'Cormac?' Sylvie opened the bedroom door but Cormac was face down on the bed and didn't turn around. 'Cormac darling.' She leant over the bed, and put a hand on his shoulder.

The moment she touched him, he erupted. 'Leave me alone! Why can't you ever just leave me alone?'

'But Cormac-'

'Go away!' he roared.

'Oh!' Sylvie stood up and turned on Robbie. 'This is all your fault! Cormac's never like this.'

'More's the pity,' Robbie murmured, letting her push past him. When she disappeared down the stairs, her long skirt flowing behind her and a muffled sob escaping her lips, he stepped into the room and shut the door. 'Why don't you just tell her you don't want to be a musician?'

Cormac didn't move.

'It's obvious you hate it.'

'No, I don't,' he said into the pillows.

'Then why do you always look so miserable?'

'I don't. It's just... hard work.' Cormac sniffled into his duvet.

'So why did you decide you were going to be a famous musician?' Robbie plonked himself down onto the beanbag.

'I didn't. It was my teacher, Mr Cunningham.'

'Your teacher?' Robbie scoffed. 'If I listened to my teachers...'

'Maybe you should. You set fire to things, steal and break things...'

'At least I don't lock myself away all day, or walk around pretending to compose music.'

'I do compose music.'

'Play me something then.'

'The piano's downstairs.'

'Use this.' Robbie reached for a tin whistle on the shelf.

Cormac sniffed a little but sat up and got off his bed. All the fight had gone out of him. He wetted his lips and blew into the whistle.

'Ow!' Robbie planted his hands over his ears.

'Just practising,' Cormac explained. Then taking a deep breath, Cormac closed his eyes and blew into the whistle once more. This time a long soft note emerged, followed by another and then another. Robbie listened in amazement as Cormac with eyes closed swayed in the centre of the room like a young tree in a breeze. His small fingers lifted gracefully up and down the thin tube like a ballerina's footsteps, releasing pure notes in a melody that made Robbie think of a kite drifting high in the sky on a summer's day.

'Hey, that was really good!' Robbie exclaimed when Cormac was finished.

Cormac opened his eyes and blinked.

'Why don't you play stuff like that all the time?'

'I'm not supposed to. Mr Cunningham says I have to learn the classical composers first.'

'Did you ever hear of Elvis Presley?'

'Course.'

'Can you play something?' Robbie sat up eagerly.

'No, but I can do Oasis.'

'Who?' But Cormac had already begun a tin whistle version of 'Don't Look Back in Anger.'

Robbie shrugged. 'It's okay.'

'Oasis are the best,' Cormac said, his eyes shining. 'Here, listen to this.' He handed Robbie the earphones of his iPod and twiddled with the screen for a moment before pressing play.

Robbie lay back on the beanbag but jumped up in shock when he heard the sound reverberating around his head. 'What the blazes?'

'The best rock group ever.'

Gingerly, Robbie reinserted the earphones. He could hear every bang of the drums, an electric guitar, some sort of keyboard, and a man's voice. It all swirled about him as if he were in a vast hall of music. 'Super!' Cormac took the other earpiece and together they listened to Cormac's favourite tunes.

CHAPTER NINETEEN

One evening Beth and Jess had a rare moment alone in the garden.

'What do you think of Robbie's mother?' Beth said.

'She's funny.' Jess giggled. 'The way she keeps staring at my clothes.'

'She doesn't approve of girls wearing trousers.'

'I know, she asked to see my skirts and nearly fainted at the length of them.'

Beth sat down on the low wall along the patio. 'She reminds me of Gran.'

Jess became quiet. 'Yeah, she makes a good dinner,'

'I hope they stay.'

'So do I.'

Beth knocked against Jess. 'You don't love him, do you?'

'Course not!' Jess blushed.

'Good. Cos he's not real.'

'Yes he is. He's warm and his heart beats,' Jess said snootily.

'It won't last, Jess.'

'Well I'm going to enjoy it while it does.'

So every day after school Jess would hurry through her homework and then hang out with Jack. He spent most of his time studying car and motorbike magazines which Jess's father bought him. 'This stuff is extraordinary. Do you know these motorbikes go from zero to sixty miles an hour in three seconds?'

'Really?' Jess feigned interest. 'Why don't we go out for a walk and spot a couple?'

'Brilliant.'

Beth watched them leave from the window. It took ages for them to walk along the street, because Jack's head swivelled with every passing car, and if a motorbike came into view he entered some sort of trance. Jess tried to tug him along but Jack stopped at every car to cup his hands against drivers' door windows and peer at dashboards. Eventually Jess took out her phone and began to scroll with a scowl on her face. Beth guessed it had dawned on Jess that Jack wasn't so wonderful after all. She sighed with relief. Robbie and his family needed to return home without any complications.

* * *

Meanwhile, Ron couldn't get the boy, Robbie, out of his head. His appearance had brought back so many memories and it seemed only last week since his beloved family disappeared. The grief was unbearable.

He shuffled about the house, completely abandoning his daily routine. No reading the paper after breakfast, no walk to the end of the street mid-morning, or nap after lunch. Instead he wandered from room to room, stopping to sit down in odd places and get cold. His favourite spot was the green velvet chair in the hall, where Robbie and Beth had helped him sit down. It was from this position that he encountered Janice on her knees scrubbing the floor.

'Who d'ya have tramping about the house?' she

complained.

Ron hadn't noticed the collection of muddy foot-prints leading across the hall from the door to the basement.

'Were you out in the garden?'

He coughed. 'A couple of children turned up here,' he said tentatively, 'I don't know who they were.'

'Him really tall and her with mousey brown hair?' Janice looked up.

'Yes,' Ron wheezed excitedly.

'I know 'em.' She nodded.

'You do?' Ron waved a shaky hand.

'Well, Gráinne does.'

'Are they her friends?'

Janice shrugged. 'They're in school together.'

Ron stared at the woman. How could he get to see those children again? He needed to establish whether Robbie might be his grandson or even great-grand-son. With the same name there was a chance they were related.

'Mrs O'Reilly,' he said, 'I'd like you to help me with something.'

* * *

Much to Beth and Robbie's immense shock, the next day at school, Gráinne issued them with an invitation. 'Mam wants you to come around to lunch,' she told them in a quiet corner of the playground.

'What?' Beth asked sure she had misheard what sounded like an invitation.

'Why?' Robbie asked.

'That old man wants to see you.'

'The one in the big house?'

'Yeah.'

'We didn't do anything wrong,' Robbie blurted.

'Only trespassed! And covered his house with mud,' Gráinne said nastily.

'Then why lunch? What's he want?'

Gráinne shrugged. 'Dunno.' She glared at them. 'But this doesn't mean we're friends, right?'

'Absolutely right,' Robbie agreed.

'Of course.' Beth nodded her head vigorously.

Gráinne walked away leaving Robbie and Beth watching her in silence.

* * *

The invitation was for the following Saturday. That morning Robbie and Beth left the house saying they would be back in the afternoon.

'Where are you going?' Isabelle asked, worried.

'To see if we can find a way home,' Robbie said innocently.

'Out there!' Isabelle peered out of the window. She still hadn't ventured beyond the house or garden.

'We won't be long.' Robbie gave her a kiss on the cheek.

'Bye,' Sylvie called down from her bedroom. She was engaged in her Saturday morning ritual of breakfast in bed. Bill was resting beside her. Normally he would have been out at his morning surgery, but the doctor had insisted that he not return to work for another month.

Beth trailed slowly along the path beside Robbie. 'It's weird. Why does he want to see us?'

'Maybe he's going to leave us his house!' Robbie grinned.

'But he doesn't even know us.'

Robbie shrugged. 'You never know. I heard of someone who met an old lady once, she died a week later and left him all her money.'

'If that happens to me, I'm going to buy the biggest library in the whole world with all my favourite books and no one will be allowed to borrow them.'

Robbie gave her a look of scorn. 'Well, I'm going to buy the fastest car in the whole world. Much faster than Jack's bike.'

Talk of wealth and riches brought them all the way to Gráinne's lane. 'How do we get in?' Beth said when they faced the large metal gate.

'It's open, look.' Robbie pushed and it swung aside.

They stepped into the courtyard. The front door had been freshly painted yellow since their last visit.

Gráinne was waiting in the doorway. 'Come on.'

Swallowing down her nerves, Beth let Robbie go first. Inside there was no sign of Gráinne's brother or mother. There were clothes, magazines and DVDs scattered all over a sofa. On a table in the kitchen area Beth spied a box of cornflakes and some dirty breakfast bowls.

Gráinne noticed Beth looking about. 'Stop gawping!'

'Oh, sorry.' Scowling Gráinne led them out of her back door through the long grass in the apple orchard up to the old house.

'Wipe your feet this time.' She pointed at a mat beside the door. Beth brushed hers vigorously. Robbie gave his a token swipe.

'I don't know why he wants to see you.'

This time there was a light on in the basement. 'Hey, what's that?' Robbie pointed at a lump in the corner covered with a large white sheet.

'Who cares?' Gráinne said crossly but Robbie pulled

off the sheet. His mouth fell open. 'It can't be…'

'What?' Beth followed him over.

'It looks just like Jack's 350cc! The one you knocked over.' Robbie grabbed the sheet and began polishing furiously. 'But it's all rusty.'

'What's he on about?' Gráinne asked.

'Dunno.' Beth was confused.

Robbie stared at the bike in amazement. 'Look it's got the same registration plate. What's it doing here?'

'Haven't a clue.' Gráinne snatched the sheet and threw it back over the bike. 'It looks as if it's about to fall apart.'

'Come on, Robbie.' Beth said anxiously. 'Let's get this over with.'

Robbie followed scratching his head.

CHAPTER TWENTY

Ron couldn't stop his stomach churning and heart racing. His doctor wouldn't be at all pleased. She'd cut out all stimulating activities when his heart had developed an irregularity, but he trusted it not to let him down this morning. Life couldn't be that unfair.

In the front room, the dinning-room table was laid for four. Ron intended to study Robbie for the duration of the meal, and planned to sit him facing the window so light would fall on his face. Ron would sit opposite. He never usually ate in the cold front room, his place was the kitchen where there was an Aga that reminded him of Isabelle, even though the inside was sadly empty of sizzling roast chickens or bubbling shepherds' pies. But he could still taste Isabelle's cooking when he closed his eyes and concentrated.

When at last Ron heard the three children enter the

hall, he wheezed himself into a standing position.

'You all right?' Janice asked gruffly, putting bottles of fizzy drinks on the table.

'Perfectly, thank you.' He tightly gripped the chair and smoothed down his tie with a free hand.

'You look a bit funny,' she persisted.

'I hear someone.' Ron craned his head in the direction of the door and just then Gráinne, Beth and Robbie appeared.

'I'm very glad you could come,' Ron said in as strong a voice he could muster. 'Please come in.'

Beth stepped forward. 'I'm very sorry about our muddy feet the other day.'

'Oh, don't worry about that.' He waved her apology away. 'It doesn't matter.'

Janice muttered something under her breath.

'Now.' Ron pointed at a place at the table. 'Robbie you sit here.' He watched the tall boy move across the room. Really the likeness was uncanny. He even wiped his nose with the back of his hand the way Robbie used to, no matter how many times Ron told him not to.

'Where will we go?' Gráinne interrupted.

'Wherever you like,' Ron said without looking at her or Beth. In fact for the whole meal he never moved his eyes away from Robbie.

'Where do you go to school?' he asked him when they were waiting for their food.

'What's it called again?' Robbie said to Beth.

'St Joseph's Primary.'

'Oh yeah.'

'You attend with girls?' Ron raised his brows.

'Yeah.' Robbie grinned.

'And are you good at school?'

Robbie blushed. 'Sometimes.'

'He's dyslexic,' Beth piped up.

'Sorry?' Ron put a hand behind his ear.

'He has difficulty reading and spelling words.'

'Oh, I see.' Ron sat back in his chair. Dyslexia. Is that what had been wrong with his poor Robbie? And could this boy have inherited it from him? 'That can't be easy,' Ron said gently.

Robbie didn't reply; he was concentrating on catching stringy cheese dangling off a pizza with slices of sausage on top.

'I had a son once who may have had the same problem …' Ron gazed into the distance, 'but I didn't know it at the time.'

The children listened politely, not really interested. Gráinne's eyes kept flicking to the screen on her mobile phone.

It seemed that no one was going to speak again until Robbie suddenly broke the silence. 'Where d'ya get that bike downstairs?'

'Eh what?' Ron came out of his daze.

'The Matchless 350.'

'Aaah.' Ron nodded and smiled. 'That belonged to my eldest son.'

'But that's my brother's bike,' Robbie said.

Ron put his napkin on the table. 'What did you say?'

'That's my brother's bike.'

'What's your brother called?'

'Jack.'

Ron couldn't answer. His head felt strange and light as if it might float away. 'Jack?' he said faintly.

'Yeah.'

'Oh dear.' Ron became so weak that he knocked his glass of water off the table and slumped sideways in his chair.

'What's wrong with him?' Beth asked, panicked.

'I dunno.' Gráinne's normal deadpan expression had been replaced with one of worry.

'Get your mother.' Robbie stood up.

Ron could hear voices about him and people moving but as it took every ounce of his energy to remain conscious, he couldn't respond. Jack! Just hearing the name caused his heart to skip several beats. He tried to focus on breathing. This event was too important. He must stay conscious.

Something hard and cold was being pressed against

his lips. 'Water,' said Janice. He pushed it away. Just a few more seconds and he would come around. Either that or he would be sick all over the floor.

'What happened?' He heard Janice ask sharply.

'We didn't touch him,' Gráinne said defensively.

'Maybe we should go,' Beth suggested.

'No!' Ron spluttered but nobody seemed to notice; there was a shuffling of chairs, some murmured, 'Thank yous,' followed by silence.

He was left alone in the cold room.

Ron gave up trying to lift his head and wept.

CHAPTER TWENTY-ONE

'That was really strange,' Beth muttered outside the front door.

'Pity we didn't get to finish lunch,' Robbie said mournfully. 'That Pisa or whatever you call it was smashing.'

'Pizza?' Beth said surprised. 'No, it wasn't that good. It was frozen. You should have a fresh one.'

'Can you make one?'

'No. We'll get takeaway. We've loads of menus at home.' It would be her money buying the pizza and Robbie had the largest appetite of anyone she'd ever met; she'd soon be out of all of her birthday and Christmas money, but seeing as he was stuck in her house with no means of going home she supposed it was only fair that she fed him.

Half an hour later, they were sitting in Beth's front room munching on freshly delivered pepperoni pizza.

Robbie had his eyes closed and strings of white moz-zarella cheese stretched from the slice of pizza to his mouth. 'Mmmm,' he moaned in ecstasy.

'I hope he doesn't die.'

'Who?' Robbie opened his eyes.

'That old man,' Beth continued. 'He's over ninety, I'd say.'

Robbie licked his lips. 'This is the most delicious piece of food ever created by God.'

Beth giggled.

Robbie finished his slice and said, 'I want to know what he was doing with Jack's Matchless 350.'

Beth frowned. 'It can't be Jack's bike. That's impos-sible!'

'It was,' Robbie insisted. 'The registration number was the same.'

Beth scooped up another slice of pizza and drips of paprika-coloured oil slithered off it. 'Well, there's nothing you can do about it.'

'We could get it out of there,' Robbie suggested.

'Oh no, you couldn't.' Beth stared at him.

'I think it's time we became friends with Gráinne.' Robbie chewed thoughtfully.

'She hates us!' Beth coughed.

'I want that bike.' Robbie's eyes glinted in the way that Beth knew always preceded trouble.

'What's that about a bike?' Jack walked into the room.

'Nothing,' Robbie lied badly. Beth blushed and looked at the floor.

'I just heard the words Matchless 350.' Jack sat down opposite Robbie.

'I thought I saw a bike that looked like your one,' Robbie said sulkily.

'Here?'

Robbie nodded, putting down his slice of pizza.

'May I?' Jack looked at Beth and, when she nodded, picked up a slice. 'Where did you see it?'

'I don't think it was it,' Robbie began.

'Tell me.' Jack wagged a finger at Robbie.

Beth looked anxiously at Robbie but he was staring moodily at the floor, so she spoke, 'We went to this old man's house.'

'Go on,' Jack encouraged.

'He invited us to lunch and Robbie thought he saw your bike in the basement.'

'Did you check the registration number?' Jack's eyes bore into Robbie.

Robbie nodded.

Jack stopped eating. 'ZJ 7005?'

Robbie nodded again.

'Well, we've got to go around there.' Jack stood up.

'The man's really old.' Beth warned.

'He might have met Dad and bought it from him.'

'Oh yeah,' Beth looked at Jack with new respect. 'You're right.'

'Of course I'm right.'

Robbie grunted something inaudible.

'Show me where he lives.' Jack strode to the door.

'We're tired,' Robbie moaned but Jack wouldn't

listen to any excuses.

'Tired? Ha!'

And so the three of them set off, Beth awkwardly leading the way, Jack slightly behind and Robbie trailing the two of them. 'Stop pretending to have an interest in nature!' Jack snapped but Robbie ignored him, stubbornly staring at every bird and stick of fauna along the way. 'Keep going,' Jack ordered Beth. 'We can leave him behind if we have to.'

But Robbie was still with them when they reached Ron's street.

'That's the one,' Beth said pointing at the house but there was an ambulance parked outside.

'Hurry up!' Jack said.

They arrived just in time to see Ron being carried out on a stretcher and Gráinne's mother, Janice, standing in the door way, her face haggard.

Ron's eyes were closed, but his head was gently rocking from side to side as if he were searching for something.

'Is he going to be all right?' Beth asked one of the ambulance men.

'Who are you?'

'Friends,' Jack said taking a step forward. 'My name is Jack Montgomery and this is my brother, Robbie.'

Suddenly Ron opened his eyes, and waved his hands erratically.

'You're all right.' The ambulance man leaned over him soothingly. 'We'll have you at the hospital in no time.'

But Ron kept fussing, twitching and turning. His feet kicked as if he wanted to get off the stretcher. Then his eyes rested on Jack and his manner changed entirely. Staring Jack straight in the eye, Ron became so still that he may have died but then he opened his lips took a long shuddering breath, his eyes rolled back in their sockets and he passed out in a faint.

'Hurry!' one ambulance man said to the other. They slid Ron into the back of the emergency vehicle. One jumped in with him while the other slammed the doors and ran around to the front. Then they moved away, lights flashing and sirens wailing.

The children stared after them in a kind of daze.

'Now what?' Beth asked.

'Where did you say the bike was?' Jack turned to her.

'In the basement,' Robbie replied.

'Is there a way in?' Jack ran down the stone steps to the basement door. It was locked. He peered in the windows. They were barred.

'We came in the back way,' Beth explained.

'I know how we can get down there,' Robbie said.

'Go on then.' Jack folded his arms.

'Beth, ring the doorbell,' Robbie instructed.

'But what will I say if Gráinne's mother answers?'

'You won't have to say anything. You'll run away before she answers. Once she comes to the front door, I'll throw a stone up the steps to distract her and Jack can slip inside.'

Jack laughed. 'I can't see that working!'

'Do you have a better idea?' Robbie asked hotly.

'Yes, I'll simply ring the doorbell and explain who I am.' Jack said smugly. 'Then she'll let me in'

'You don't know Gráinne's mother,' Beth warned. 'And anyway why would she let you in?'

'Yeah,' Robbie sniggered. 'Just because you think you're somebody special at home doesn't mean anything now.'

Jack frowned. 'Oh.'

'I know.' Beth blushed scarlet. 'Let's say we forgot something and have come back to get it.'

'Yes, good one.' The boys agreed so all three trooped up the steps to the large wooden door. It had a round white button for the bell in the centre. Beth was just about to press it when she saw that the door wasn't fully closed. She pointed at the open crack. 'Gráinne's mother must have forgotten to close it.'

'Brilliant.' Robbie pushed forward.

The house felt hollow and silent. A smell of onions lingered from lunch and the only sound was the large grandfather clock ticking in the empty hall.

Jack whistled. 'This is quite a place.'

Ignoring him, Beth and Robbie walked to the door at the back of the hall that lead to the basement. They felt their way down the first few steps until Beth found the light switch. 'There.' She pointed at a mound under a sheet.

Robbie dashed over, but Jack was the first to reach the sheet. His face fell when he whipped it away. 'It's ruined.'

Beth could understand what he was feeling. The red paint that had gleamed on the body of the engine was a dull powdery pink. Rust covered every spot of metal that wasn't painted and the rubber covers on the handlebars and throttle were completely worn away. 'This can't be it,' Jack whispered.

'Look.' Robbie pointed at the registration plate.

Jack squinted at the digits. Even in the bad light there could be no dispute: it was his bike. 'I paid one hundred pounds for this. Now it's useless. What's it doing here?' He gazed at the rubble in the dark room.

Then his eyes fell on something else. 'Isn't that Dad's toolbox?'

Robbie followed Jack's gaze to a long metal box, thick with rust. 'No, his was blue.'

'The paint's gone.' Jack attempted to prize it open. 'Help me.' The two of them banged and pushed at the box until they eventually forced it open.

'Look!' Jack said excitedly. 'His compass!' He picked up a small circular object. 'I'm sure this is it.'

'These are his pliers,' Robbie said. 'See the handle's still missing a piece.'

'What's Dad's stuff doing here?' Jack became pale.

'You don't think…' Beth began but then stopped.

'What?' Robbie and Jack said in unison.

'Well, he's got your bike and your father's toolbox…'

'Yes.'

'Could he be some sort of relative?'

Jack walked over to the steps and sat on the very last one. 'We've got to check the rest of the house,' he said. 'Find out what else he's got.'

'But we can't!' Beth panicked. 'What'll we do if Gráinne's mum sees us?'

'One of us can keep watch downstairs.' Jack pinned his eyes on her. 'You.'

Beth swallowed. The last thing she wanted was to be left alone downstairs. Gráinne might walk in and see her. What would she say to her? Things had become increasingly odd since Beth found out that Gráinne's father had died. Gráinne no longer teased her and they had reached an awkward truce.

'We won't be long,' Jack assured her.

Two minutes later Beth stood in the hall watching Jack and Robbie hurry up the large wooden staircase. When they were gone, she peeked her head into the dining room. The lunch table had been cleared and moved back against the wall. She stepped inside and weaved her way through mismatched armchairs and oddly sized side tables to the window. From there it was as if she were floating several feet above the road. She saw the tops of people's heads as they passed by and the shiny roofs of cars which had stopped in the traffic.

What must it be like for that old man to live in this huge house alone? She shivered and turned to face the mantelpiece. A selection of framed photographs stood in a row. She'd noticed them at lunch, but they were too far away to see properly. She carefully picked one up. It was a black and white photograph of a young man wearing a dark suit with a floppy white collar. He had a large nose, and black hair slicked against his head with a side parting. In tiny writing below she read the digits 1938. Wow! The picture was ancient. The next one was a group photograph. A woman, with wavy dark hair, was wearing a long winter coat that looked beige although it could have been any pale colour, and a matching hat. An old fashioned pram stood beside her and a tall good-looking man with a straight back. He looked similar to the man in the previous photograph except now he had a moustache and flecks of grey in his hair. The woman reminded

Beth a little of Robbie's mother but it was probably her clothes and hairstyle that made her think that.

Rhythmic creaking on the stairs informed Beth that the boys were coming back so she hurried into the hall to meet them.

'We found nothing.' Robbie sighed.

'Only a huge mahogany wardrobe like Mum and Dad's and a couple of chest of drawers but anyone could have them,' Jack said looking fed up. 'We may as well go.'

They pulled the front door and plodded down the street leaving the tall empty house behind them.

* * *

When Ron woke up that afternoon, he thought he was dreaming. He'd often dreamt of waking to absolute nothingness. After all nothingness represented his life. He groaned as his eyes focused on a white empty space and a strip of fluorescent light beaming down. Maybe he had died, he thought. Oh please don't let this be it. If his family weren't in heaven, which they didn't seem to be, he didn't want to be there either.

'There, there now. You're all right,' said a soft voice.

Through fuzzy vision Ron made out a pretty nurse with a pile of auburn hair. 'You had a bad turn but you're all right.'

'What happened?' he croaked.

'You were having your lunch but you didn't feel so well.'

Ron couldn't remember a thing.

'You're going to stay with us for a couple of days,' she said tucking in his sheets.

'Oh all right,' Ron said faintly. Perhaps this wouldn't be so bad. It certainly beat his cold empty house and Janice's unhappy face at breakfast.

CHAPTER TWENTY-TWO

Jack, Robbie and Beth arrived home just in time to meet Isabelle venturing out the front door for the first time. 'I'm going down to the corner shop,' she said her voice wavering. 'I can't stick being inside a moment longer.'

'Good for you Mum.' Jack gave her a pat on the shoulder.

'You lot survive your little trips, why shouldn't I?' She laughed nervously.

It was at that moment it struck Beth that Robbie's mother looked extremely like the woman in the photo.

'Where did you get those clothes?' she blurted.

'They're mine,' Isabelle clutched her at coat.

'But you never wore them before.'

'I arrived in them but I haven't worn them since as I haven't been outside.'

Beth studied Isabelle's hair. It was dark and curled

to the chin, just like the woman's in the photo. She had the same heavy nose and, looking down Beth noticed Robbie's mother's ankles – she didn't have any. Her calves went in a straight line all the way to her feet. No ankles were visible. That couldn't be a coincidence.

'What did you say your father's name was?' Beth asked.

'My father?' Isabelle asked puzzled. 'George.'

'No, Robbie's.'

'Ron.' Isabelle reached into her sleeve for a hand-kerchief. The mere mention of her husband's name made her cry.

'What was the old man called again?' Beth whipped around to Robbie.

He frowned. 'The old geezer?'

'Robbie, I'm serious!'

'Dunno. Gráinne never told us.'

'Well, we've got to find out.'

'Why?'

'Because,' Beth said trying to keep her voice steady,

'I think he might be your Dad.'

There was an explosion of 'Poppycock!' and 'Don't be ridiculous!'

'Those photos I was looking at, they were of her,' she pointed at Isabelle, 'and maybe one of you in a pram.'

'What? Why didn't you tell us when we were there?' Jack exploded, red in the face.

'I've only just realised it.'

Isabelle gripped Beth's arm. 'Tell me exactly what you saw in the picture.'

As best as she could Beth described the woman standing beside the man and the pram at the door of a house.

'Was he incredibly handsome?' Isabelle's large violet eyes searched Beth's.

'Eh....' Beth didn't have a clue. How could a man from the last century be described as handsome? But he was tall and not hideous so she supposed he must be. 'Yeah.'

'Oh, it's Ron! You wonderful, wonderful girl!' Robbie's mother embraced her.

'It wasn't Dad!' Robbie argued. 'This man is ancient!'

'Of course he is!' Beth said exasperated. 'It makes sense.'

Beth grabbed Isabelle's arm. 'You must go see him!'

Robbie was mutinous. 'It isn't Dad!'

But Beth was jumping up and down with excitement. 'Don't you see? That's why he asked you to lunch! And,' she gazed into space as something else struck her. 'It was when you mentioned Jack's name that he passed out.'

'Is that true?' Jack asked his brother.

'Maybe,' Robbie admitted reluctantly.

Beth was more and more certain that her assumption was correct. 'He fainted on the stretcher when he saw you, Jack! It's got to be him.'

'Well, why didn't he just say so?' Robbie snarled. 'He's met me twice. If that was my Dad he would have—'

'Maybe he couldn't believe it,' Jack said thinking

hard. 'I mean we hardly can.'

'Oh stop babbling!' Isabelle wailed. 'Where is he?'

'We've got to find out which hospital he's in,' Beth said chewing her lip.

'Ring 'em up,' Jack suggested.

'And ask them if they have a one hundred year old man?'

'No, ask for Ron Montgomery. If they say yes, we've found Dad.'

Beth sprinted into the house and informed her mother what was happening. Sylvie picked up the telephone and rang St James's Hospital. The receptionist said, 'Yes, a Ron Montgomery had been brought in that afternoon and was currently in the ICU.

'What does that mean?' Isabelle said pale as ghost.

'The Intensive Care Unit,' Sylvie explained.

'Oh God, I thought it meant the morgue,' Isabelle said shaking.

'I'll drive you,' Sylvie said.

'Thank you!' Isabelle clasped Sylvie's hand.

'Come on.' Sylvie grabbed her keys from the hook in the hall and they all followed her outside. Just as they were about to get into the car, Jess and Cormac appeared at the front door wanting to know what was going on.

'There's no time to explain,' Beth said opening a door. 'Get Dorothea.'

Moments later Dorothea stumbled out of the house with a puffy red face. Clearly she'd been in the middle of an afternoon nap – sharing a bed with her mother meant she got very little sleep. Robbie bundled her into the back seat next to Beth and Jack. His mother took the front passenger seat beside Sylvie.

'Fast as you can!' Isabelle said.

'I'll do my best,' Sylvie replied backing out of the drive.

The journey across the city took thirty minutes but it seemed a lot longer as Robbie's mother kept whimpering in terror. 'Everything's so frightening!' she exclaimed and leaning over to look at the speedometer she gasped, 'We're going 80!' Isabelle closed her eyes. 'Oh Lord!'

When they arrived at the hospital, Sylvie told everyone to get out while she parked. Beth chose to remain. She gazed out of the window at the grey hulk of building. A sign stating Entrance shone harshly over the main door. Trickles of people were migrating towards it. Most were frowning, tired and hungry looking. It was seven o'clock. Past dinner time.

Rows of pale yellow windows glowed weakly, and Beth imagined patients lying in beds within. In some she spotted the flicker of a brisk nurse passing, in others the blue-white reflection of a television, probably showing the boring news or Coronation Street: the worst programmes.

* * *

Eventually Sylvie was satisfied with the position of the car and instructed Beth to get out. Reluctantly Beth pushed open the door and pulled up the hood of her jacket. It had started to rain. The car park seemed to stretch for miles. Nearly every space was full. It was as if every person in Dublin had someone to visit, someone to miss their dinner for, and someone to lie awake at night worrying about.

CHAPTER TWENTY-THREE

When they all reached the hospital reception area, Isabelle bustled ahead. 'Where's my husband? We haven't a moment to lose!'

'We're looking for Ron Montgomery,' Jack explained to the confused receptionist.

'Oh.' She blushed. 'I'll just check for you.' She keyed Ron's name into a computer. 'He's in the ICU unit on the third floor.'

'The third floor.' Isabelle darted from one side of reception to the other like an anxious hen.

'I'm afraid you can't go up there now.'

'Can't?' Isabelle turned on her like a Rhinoceros about to charge.

'Well, eh… it's not usual.'

'Madam, there is nothing usual about this situation.'

'Please.' Jack intervened, flashing his most charming smile. 'Just a few moments.'

The receptionist's shoulders dropped. 'Well you can try...'

'Thank you.' Jack briskly led the others along a maze of corridors lined with windows looking out onto more hospital buildings.

'It's more like a city than a hospital!' Isabelle gaped.

'Keep going, Mum.' Jack kept a firm grip on her arm.

Beth walked slightly behind with Robbie and Dorothea who kept stumbling as she tried to keep up.

'Here we are at last,' Jack said when they stood before a large green sign stating Intensive Care Unit.

A young woman wearing a blue uniform, with auburn hair piled into a high ponytail, came out of double doors.

'Oh please, you've got to help us.' Isabelle rushed up to her.

The nurse took Isabelle's hand and smiled gently at her. 'I will don't worry.'

'It's my husband.'

The nurse nodded. 'Tell me his name.'

'Ron Montgomery.'

The nurse looked puzzled. 'Montgomery. Are you sure?'

'Of course!' Isabelle bleated, 'We've got to see him.'

'What's your name please?'

'Isabelle, and these are my children, Jack, Robbie and Dorothea.'

'One moment.' The nurse hurried back through the double doors.

'It's not Dad!' Robbie said urgently to his mother. 'I'm telling you! Wait until you see him. It can't be!'

'Do not speak to me!' Isabelle stared resolutely at the double doors.

She didn't have to wait long; they swung open again and the nurse reappeared. 'Yes, you can come in.'

Suddenly Isabelle was reluctant to move; Jack had to push her along a squeaky polished floor, past beds surrounded by high tech machinery with flashing lights and beeping noises. At the end of the ward the young nurse stood waiting.

'Ten minutes only I'm afraid and I'll have to ask you to leave.'

Isabelle edged closer to the bed. 'Ron, darling, is that you? Ron?' she whispered.

The old man opened his eyes and taking one look at Isabelle's violet eyes and halo of dark hair, a shudder began in his stomach, rippled through his chest and erupted out of his mouth, 'Isabelle!'

'Oh, Ron, is that really you?' She reached for his hand, tears spilling onto her cheeks.

'Isabelle,' he repeated exhausted.

Robbie's mother began babbling a series of questions. She wanted to know where he'd been. What had happened to him? Why he was so frail and, well, old?

'Sixty years,' was all he could manage, tears streaming down his cheeks.

Isabelle turned to Jack. 'What's he talking about? I don't understand.'

Jack shook his head. 'I don't know, Mum.'

Beth pushed her way forward. It wasn't like her to speak out in a group and certainly not in such a close grief-stricken one as this family circle but she had to point out the obvious; what no one else seemed to be able to accept. This ancient man must be their father. 'He was left behind. Don't you see?' She stared around at them all. 'He must be over one hundred now.' She fixed her gaze on Isabelle. 'When was he born?'

Isabelle dabbed a handkerchief to her forehead. '1911,' she said faintly and then with more determination, 'Yes. 1911, two years before me.'

Beth's eyes opened large. 'That means he's…' She thought for a moment.

'One hundred and eight years old,' Jack finished for her. 'Don't be ridiculous. Our father is in his forties. He's got black hair and he works in the bank. This man isn't him!'

'Told you,' Robbie chimed in.

Oh, if only they could understand but it was so difficult. Ron looked nothing like he used to. Beth wouldn't have believed anyone who told her that this ancient grey-haired frail man was her father either. 'Ask him questions. Only things he could know!'

The family shuffled closer around the bed, leaving Beth against the wall.

Jack moved closer to the bed. 'Eh … this might sound a little strange, but we live in number 3 Hawthorn Road or at least we used to, but something happened and we ended up here.' Ron seemed barely to be listening. He kept looking from Isabelle's face to each of his children's. 'And we don't know how to get back again,' Jack finished looking about awkwardly.

'Oh, I'll do it.' Robbie pushed himself forward angrily. 'Do you remember me?' he demanded.

Ron nodded. 'Robbie,' he said softly.

'Look, my friend thinks that just cos you've the same name as our father, you are him.'

'I am.' Ron attempted to smile although it was hard to tell, as his mouth was so wrinkled and wobbly.

'Right, that's it.' Isabelle flapped them all away. 'Ron

needs his rest. I shall stay here with him. Go home!'

* * *

Of course, Ron Montgomery believed that he had died and finally gone to heaven. His beloved wife, young and utterly beautiful, stood before him. Dorothea's dark anxious eyes looked at him from the end of the bed. Jack stood tall and concerned, and Robbie was there too, looking sulky and angry over something as usual. All of them looked exactly as they had done the day they disappeared and Ron presumed that he must be young again too. But something caught Ron's eye that wasn't quite right. The girl, the one Robbie had brought to lunch, was standing slightly apart from the group watching awkwardly. What was she doing there? Surely if he were in heaven she wouldn't be there too? Ron closed his eyes. It was all too confusing and difficult to think about.

* * *

Later that evening, Isabelle returned home by taxi – Sylvie had given her the money – and entered the kitchen pale and tired.

'Would you like something to eat?' Jess asked.

'Oh, thank you, dear, but I'm not hungry.'

'You should eat something,' Jack pressed her.

'Mum, made soup,' Jess said. 'Holding out a pot.'

'Oh!' Isabelle looked surprised.

'I'm not completely useless, you know.' Sylvie uncurled herself from the sofa. 'I insist you eat. You look terrible.'

'I don't know what's wrong with me.' Isabelle's face crumpled. 'I've got my Ron back but...'

'There, there. You eat up now. Here's some nice crusty bread to go with it.' Sylvie put a plate before Isabelle.

Beth watched her mother in amazement. It had been shock enough, when earlier that evening she'd pulled out a cookery book and instructed Jess and Beth to chop carrots, potatoes, peppers, garlic and onions while she familiarised herself with the herbs and spices inherited from her mother's kitchen. The result was a perfectly acceptable minestrone soup, which everyone enjoyed, including Isabelle once she'd mopped her eyes and settled down.

'We'll move in with him, of course,' Isabelle said when she'd finished eating.

'Move in with who?' Robbie asked.

'Your father.'

'We're not living with him!' Robbie's bowl of soup slopped all over the wooden table. 'We're going home!' Beth guessed Robbie had meant it as a demand but his voice broke and it came out sounding more like a plea.

'But darling we don't know how to get home,' Isabelle said, lost and miserable.

'We don't have a choice,' Jack sighed into his soup. 'We have to go.'

Beth looked at the unhappy faces about the table and whispered, 'We'll all still be friends,' but nobody was listening to her.

And so the following day, Robbie and his family

collected their belongings – which amounted to no more than the clothes they were wearing – to walk the few miles across town to Ron's home. Sylvie offered to drive them but Isabelle said that she'd done too much for them already

'It was nothing,' Sylvie said, generous now that their enforced stay was over.

'But do all come to dinner on Sunday,' Isabelle said. 'It's the least I can do to repay you for your hospitality.'

Afterwards Jess went upstairs to sort out her room and Cormac disappeared into the front room to the piano. Everything was returning to normal. But it couldn't be normal for Robbie and his family, thought Beth. How would they survive in that big house with their father almost dead in hospital? Beth felt terribly guilty; if only she hadn't insisted on going to school with Robbie that day. His family would never have chased after him and would all still be happy and healthy together in the last century.

CHAPTER TWENTY-FOUR

Beth called around most Saturdays to see Robbie. They weren't in school together anymore as he had returned to the modern-day Sandford Park, and so she caught up with him at the weekends. He told her Jack had been accepted into Trinity College Dublin by convincing the authorities that he'd gone to school somewhere in England and all of his school reports and exam results had been burnt in a fire. According to Jack they were charmed by his good looks – Robbie rolled his eyes – and excellent diction so they overlooked the usual bureaucratic rules and opened their fine oak doors.

Isabelle settled into running Seabury, her new home. She kept on Janice to help her, but also enjoyed her washing machine, dishwasher, Hoover and food mixer. 'I never knew housework could be so easy!' she told Beth delighted with the gadgets. 'And the local delicatessens are marvellous!' She was less keen on the supermarkets. The first time she attempted to shop in a supermarket she'd returned home to bed with a headache. 'It was like a factory. I didn't know what anything was! And the vegetables taste of chemicals and all those exotic fruits from far away countries!' As for the high street shops, she simply couldn't understand the fashions. She thought the clothes were ill-fitting and badly made. 'Why are the girls so thin? The poor things look malnourished.'

While Isabelle babbled away to her, Beth noticed that Robbie was more subdued than he used to be. He said the school was different now. 'There's about two hundred students and I don't know any of them,' he complained.

'Of course you don't.' Beth giggled.

'And we're in this new building. I don't know my way around.'

'And what about the school work?' Beth ventured.

'It's okay.' Robbie kicked his desk. 'I'm doing extra

stuff.'

'With a special teacher?'

'Did you know loads of famous scientists and engineers are dyslexic?'

'I told you that!' Beth laughed.

Robbie didn't join in. 'When I leave school, I'm going to figure out a way to time-travel.'

'Do you still want to go back?'

'I want my Dad back.'

It was the first time Robbie had mentioned Ron since visiting him in hospital.

'How's he doing?'

'All right, I suppose.'

'Maybe he'll come home soon.'

'Maybe,' Robbie agreed, without conviction.

* * *

However Ron was released from hospital, not long afterwards.

'You're doing great these days,' said the nurse with the red hair on his last day, 'like a new man!'

'Thanks to your wonderful care and my wife's visits.'

'She's certainly devoted.'

'As am I.' Ron chuckled.

'Now, no overdoing it,' the nurse warned. 'Lots of bed rest when you get home.'

'Why?' Ron laughed. 'What am I saving myself for?'

'I want you to reach your next birthday,' the nurse said, discreetly wiping away a tear.

That evening, Ron arrived home by ambulance. Isabelle, together with Janice, had scrubbed the entire house from top to bottom, and Jack, Robbie and Dorothea stood in a line in the hall to welcome him. All three of them wore brave faces and smiles.

'Welcome home, darling.' Isabelle immediately tucked Ron's blanket around his knees and tightened his dressing gown. 'I've the fire lit.'

'It's June!' Ron protested.

'You've to keep warm,' Isabelle said firmly and pushed his chair into the front room.

That evening, Ron wiggled his toes contently by

the fire and studied his family around him. Of course the situation was far from ideal. He wasn't his young strong self, and they weren't all together in Hawthorn Road, which he now knew had been the happiest days of his life, but they were all together again and that was all that mattered. He still couldn't understand how his family had disappeared and turned up sixty years later looking exactly the same, but he was learning to accept it. There was so much that he didn't understand about life and he only made his mind unwell trying to do so. Much better not to fret, and anyway he had so much to be grateful for. He was still alive, and his excellent pension meant that now he had plenty with which to support his family.

'I want to hear all about what you've been up to?' Ron looked at each of them in turn. 'Dorothea, we'll start with you.'

Dorothea moved closer to her father. She used to sit on his knee when telling him her stories, but this time she hesitated. Isabelle pulled a footstool close to Ron's wheelchair. 'Here, Dorothea.'

'School's okay,' Dorothea said in a quiet voice. 'I'm playing tennis and the racquets are huge.'

Ron chuckled. 'Yes, no more wooden frames.'

'The court looks like grass,' Dorothea frowned, 'but it's not.'

'Our rugby pitch is the same,' Robbie said with disgust. 'Fake.'

'But no more muddy boots for your mother to clean.' Ron smiled.

'There's grass in Trinity,' Jack piped up.

Ron looked at his eldest with pride. 'How's it going in there?'

'Good.'

'Good boy. I always knew you'd go far.'

'I'm going to be a scientist,' Robbie interrupted.

'Wonderful. An excellent profession.'

'Now, that's enough for today.' Isabelle took hold of Ron's wheelchair. 'Your father has to rest.'

'No, Isabelle.' Ron reached a hand over his shoulder

to pat hers. 'I've waited a long time for this.'

Isabelle sighed. 'But the nurse said you needed rest.'

'And I will, tomorrow.'

So Ron spent a long evening listening to Dorothea telling him what it was really like at school. 'I hate the girls, Daddy, and I don't understand them. I can't even pronounce their names: Kylie, Britney, Megan. I've never heard of any of them and they all laugh at my name.'

He then listened to Robbie explaining how he was getting lots of support and how lots of famous and very important people were dyslexic.

Ron laid a hand on Robbie's shoulder. 'I'm so sorry I didn't understand how difficult things were for you. I'm very proud of you.'

Robbie nodded, his face redder than usual. Finally Ron listened to Jack relating how he found the girls at university rather alarming, 'They're always making fun of me,' he grumbled.

'That's a good sign,' Ron said smiling. 'Take it

from me.'

* * *

Much later, at about eleven o'clock, Jack was explaining how today maths theorems were exactly the same as the ones he had been taught at school, when Ron's head suddenly dropped to one side and his whole body began shaking.

'Daddy! Daddy!' Dorothea grasped his thin arm.

'What's wrong with him?' Robbie looked up at Jack.

Jack shook his head. 'Get Mum!'

Robbie thundered down the stone steps to the kitchen where his mother was making hot chocolate. 'It's Dad!'

'What?' Isabelle dropped a spoon of chocolate powder all over the counter and dashed after him. 'Ron!' She ran to her husband. The frail old head, resting on his chest, had become completely still. 'He's not breathing! Call an ambulance!' Isabelle screeched. But before anyone could do anything the doorway to the hall shifted slightly to the right. 'What was that?

Isabelle screeched.

'The walls are moving!' Jack yelled.

'What?' Robbie glanced about. Jack was right. It was as if their dining room were in a spinning wheel.

'What's happening?' Dorothea clung to her mother.

'Hang on to something!' Jack yelled clutching the back of his father's wheelchair.

Robbie grabbed the leg of a table, Isabelle held onto the mantelpiece and wrapped her other arm around Dorothea. Ron's head remained flopped, lifeless against his chest.

'I feel sick, Mummy.' Dorothea sobbed.

Isabelle didn't answer. The turning was becoming faster and faster. Then a stroke of inspiration seemed to hit Isabelle. She dragged Dorothea across the room and shouted to them all. 'Hold on to your father's chair!'

Robbie dived towards his father's wheelchair and wrapped both hands around the thin metal leg. 'Don't let go!' Isabelle's voice echoed into the swirling room as the whooshing wind whipped their bodies higher and higher. 'Don't let go!'

All four of them held on tight to the chair, their bodies flying outwards in a circle. Dorothea's dark eyes were huge and frightened, Robbie lips wobbled so violently that he clamped them shut. 'What's that smell?' Jack shouted.

Robbie sniffed the air. He couldn't smell anything.

'Chicken!' Isabelle said looking around wildly, 'Stuffed with garlic and lemon.'

Robbie stared up at his mother. She'd finally lost her mind.

'Roast Chicken.' Ron lifted his head.

Robbie gaped. It was impossible. Thick black hair had grown over his father's bald patch, his cheeks were smooth and full, and his smile revealed straight shiny teeth.

'Dad?' Robbie asked in amazement and they all landed with a thump.

'Lunchtime!' Ron jumped to his feet, pulling his

twisted waistcoat into place.

'Oh Lord!' Isabelle was on her hands and knees.

'Let me help you.' Ron held out a hand.

Isabelle stared. 'Ron?'

'Of course!' He rubbed her arm affectionately.

'Children?' Isabelle's voice wavered.

'We're okay.' Jack pulled Dorothea to her feet, and nodded at Robbie.

Robbie studied his father. 'Are you all right?'

'Me?' Ron look puzzled. 'Why of course I'm alright.'

'But Seabury Road,' Isabelle whispered, 'and the hospital.'

'Hospital? What are you talking about?' Ron rubbed his stomach. 'Let's eat!'

'Robbie, quick.' Jack turned to his brother. 'Run outside.'

Robbie ran into the hall, which looked exactly like the small narrow one in his old home in Hawthorn Road and nothing like the large spacious one in Seabury, and flung open the front door. 'Dad's Morris

Minor is in the drive,' he called, 'there's a Daimler in Fitzgeralds' and a Ford Anglia across the road at Murphy's.'

'No BMWs or Hondas?'

Robbie returned puce-faced. 'No.'

'You know what that means,' Jack said looking around. 'We're home. We've back in the 1950s.'

On Saturday Beth visited Seabury as usual, but instead of finding Robbie, the house was full of strangers. 'What's going on?' she asked Janice, who was bossing men around as if she owned the place.

'The old man's gone.'

'What do you mean gone?' Beth stared at her stupidly. 'Gone where?'

'Dunno.'

'What about Robbie?'

Janice shrugged. 'They've all disappeared.'

'No, they can't have.' Beth ran into the dining room. 'I only saw them last Saturday.'

'Yeah, and on Wednesday, the lot of them vanished.'

Janice didn't seem too upset about it. In fact it soon became apparent that she was moving her family's belongings into the old house. 'Someone's got to look after the place,' she explained, 'there's no point in us living out the back if we don't have to.'

'But they'll be back,' Beth insisted.

Janice shrugged. 'Maybe, maybe not.'

* * *

As it turned out Robbie and his family never did come back.

Beth returned every Saturday for weeks. 'I'd give up, if I were you,' Janice said arms folded on the doorstep. 'Anyway, if they turn up, Gráinne can tell you at school.' Beth wasn't so sure about that. Even though Gráinne didn't tease her at school anymore, they weren't exactly friends.

'Where could they have gone?' Beth asked every member of her family in turn.

'I don't know,' Sylvie sighed. 'I mean they weren't exactly normal. God knows where they've ended up.'

'Maybe they went back to where they came from,' Jess suggested.

'But how? They would've had to come through here and we would've seen them!'

Jess shrugged. 'I dunno.'

And as the months past Jess and the rest of the family lost interest in Robbie and his family. But Beth still had Dorothea's diary, and she read it over and over to keep Robbie alive.

Then one day, Gráinne invited Beth to Seabury along with the whole class for lunch.

'It's not your house.'

'Please come,' Gráinne said quietly.

'Why?' Beth asked.

'Cos you never told about the lies I told at school.' Gráinne blushed. 'It was nice of you. Especially after all the things I did to you.'

'I'm sorry about your dad.'

Gráinne's eyes filled with tears and she turned her face away.

'My Gran died last year. That's why we moved here.'

'You're from London, aren't you?'

'That's where I lived, yes.'

'I've been really jealous of you.'

'Me?' Beth squeaked.

'With your posh accent and everything. And your Mum's an actress, isn't she?'

'Yeah.'

'We used to live in a really big house. I wasn't making that up.'

'It must be really hard.'

Gráinne keeps her head down. 'I can help with your Irish if you like.'

Beth couldn't believe what she was hearing. 'What?'

'You're rubbish at it.' Gráinne smiled, but it wasn't a nasty one. 'Actually, that's what really annoyed me about you, when you first came here. You're so good at everything.'

'No, I'm not –'

'You're clever and you're always top of the class.'

Beth didn't know what to say.

'I used to be like you, before…' Gráinne gulped. 'Before Dad.'

Beth linked her arm with Gráinne's. 'I'd love help

with my Irish, thanks.'

* * *

After that Gráinne did her best to hang out with Beth as much as possible. She had decided that she wanted to do well at school again and began copying the way Beth organised her books in her school bag and took down her homework, using red pen for the subject title and blue or black for the instructions. She asked Beth to check her homework before she handed it up, and corrected Beth's Irish for her. It felt good to have a friend again, not that anyone would ever replace Aisha.

It was late one afternoon, shortly after Beth had arrived home from school and was in her room texting Aisha, when a small Nissan Micra pulled up outside the house. It was the typical car that old ladies drive and Beth didn't take much notice of it. Aisha was texting about a new boy at school, who she swore was a pain but who she managed to mention whenever they talked. A short delicate woman stepped out of the small car and looked up at their house. She had auburn hair in a loose bun, small dark eyes, and wore several scarves wrapped around her neck. One of Mum's cronies, Beth thought, and turned her back to the window.

Moments later the doorbell rang, followed by the sound of Jess's feet thundering up the stairs. 'Someone to see you!' She burst into Beth's room.

'Me?' Beth put down her phone.

'Yeah, a lady called Dorothea Musgrove?' Jess tittered.

Beth looked out of the window.

'She's in the hall.'

Beth sighed and told Aisha she'd text her later.

Feeling rather cross at having her conversation interrupted – Aisha had been about to admit that she fancied this boy – Beth stomped down the stairs.

'Hello.' The woman stood up from where she'd been sitting on the sofa. 'I'm Dorothea.' She held out her hand.

'Eh … hi.' Beth shook it briefly.

'You don't remember me?' The woman's eyes twinkled. Were they tears?

Beth blushed. 'Eh … did you used to live in London?'

'No, I never lived in London.'

'Well, I'm sorry.' Beth lifted her shoulders. 'Maybe you've got the wrong person.'

'Oh, no,' the woman smiled. 'You're the right person, and,' she looked about the room, 'this is the right house.'

There was something about the way she looked just then that jolted Beth's memory. 'What did you say your name was?'

'Dorothea.'

'Dorothea what?'

'Musgrove.'

'Oh.' Beth's shoulders drooped.

The woman took a step forward. 'But I used to be called Dorothea Montgomery.'

Beth stopped breathing.

'Yes.' The woman nodded. 'And I had two brothers; one called Jack and the other–'

'Robbie,' Beth whispered.

'Yes.' There were definitely tears in her eyes now. 'Do you mind if I sit down?'

Beth shook her head. This little old woman was skinny, shy Dorothea? No way!

'We used to live in this house,' she paused, 'and for a time we lived here with your family. Do you remember?'

Luckily there was an armchair behind Beth, into which she fell backwards.

'I've been meaning to come and visit you for a long time.'

'How long?' This was too weird. The Dorothea Beth knew was younger than she was, this woman looked as old as her grandmother, no older.

'Well, we couldn't come for a very long time, and then when we could we had to wait, or at least I did.' Dorothea dabbed at her eyes. Yes, she was more like _orothea now. She was always a bit of a crybaby.

'I tried to find out everything I could.' Beth sat up. 'Nobody's ever heard of Isabelle and Ron Montgomery. It's as if you never existed!'

'Oh we existed.' Dorothea smiled in that gentle way. 'But we wouldn't have been easy to track down.'

'What happened? Where did you disappear to six months ago?'

Dorothea laughed. 'Don't you mean over sixty years ago?'

'I don't know.' Beth rubbed her temples.

'Do you remember Dad was coming out of hospital?'

'Yes,' Beth said.

'Well, he came home on a Wednesday evening, and we all sat around the fire in Seabury. You remember that house?'

'Course.' Sure she was only at Gráinne's, that afternoon.

'Well, we were chatting and then late in the night

Dad passed out. Mum thought he had died.' Dorothea's large loop earrings banged gently against her cheeks. 'It's hard to explain what happened next. None of us really knows. The whole room went into a kind of spin and we didn't know what was happening until we found ourselves back here in our old home and it was the 1950s again.'

'But that's incredible.'

'I know! Robbie spent his whole life trying to figure it out – he wanted to come back, you see, but the crack in the kitchen wall was gone. It was completely smooth as if it had never been there. Robbie tried banging the wall with a hammer. He even tried to cause an explosion but nothing worked. In the end he gave up.'

Beth blushed. She'd had a terrifying thought. Was Robbie sitting in the car outside? She would have to meet him – Robbie as an old man – she didn't think she could bear it. 'What did you do?' Beth whispered.

Dorothea shrugged and smiled. 'We got on with our lives. Dad was a young man again, and Mum went _ʌ to cooking in the kitchen, but she'd changed. Spending time with your mother had an effect on her. She set up her own business providing high quality ready-made meals. It was called Easy Entertaining. She ended up employing loads of people. Her meals were a huge success. Dad was able to give up working in the bank, which he hated, and became an artist. Actually I followed in his footsteps.'

'You're a painter?'

'Yes.' Dorothea beamed. 'Some of my paintings are even hanging in the National Gallery.'

'Wow!' Beth gaped at her. 'What about Robbie and boarding school?'

Dorothea shook her head. 'He told his teachers about dyslexia. Of course they'd never heard of it but they researched it in libraries and were able to help him. He became a scientist, just like he said he would. He helped develop the first mobile phones and digital television in Ireland.'

Where was he now? Beth didn't dare ask. How

could she possibly talk to a grown up Robbie?

Dorothea leaned forward. 'You're probably wondering why he isn't here with me.'

'Well…kind of.'

Dorothea wiped her eyes, which had suddenly filled again. 'Robbie died, just over a month ago.'

'Died?' Beth was suddenly stripped of all worries about meeting an old man. Robbie gone forever. No.

Dorothea smiled sadly. 'He became very ill about six months ago. We'd hoped he would recover but it wasn't to be.'

'But why did you leave it so long?' Beth was suddenly furious. 'Why didn't you come sooner?'

'We couldn't.' Dorothea lifted her hands. 'We had to wait until we'd past the time when we'd stayed with you.'

'Why? Why did you have to wait?'

'Because we might have met ourselves. Can you imagine, at eight years old, meeting yourself when you're an old woman?'

Beth shuddered. 'But you disappeared ages ago.'

'Yes, and we wanted to come as soon as it was exactly the time when we'd spun back in time, but that was when Robbie got sick and I was waiting for him to get better.' She looked down at her lap and Beth saw tears splash onto her wrists. Dorothea had always adored Robbie.

'He gave me this for you.' Dorothea pulled a crumpled envelope out of her bag.

Beth's name was written on it in a hand she didn't recognise. 'Did he write this?'

'No. He was too sick so I did. He told me what to say. He knew he wasn't going to get better.'

Sylvie's head suddenly popped into the room. 'Everything okay, Beth?' She looked curiously at the older woman whose mascara was running down her cheeks.

'Mum, this is Dorothea.'

'Hello, Dorothea,' Sylvie said confused.

'Robbie's sister,' Beth explained. 'You remember him?'

'Robbie?' Sylvie's voice rose and she studied the older woman again. 'Dorothea?'

Dorothea gulped and nodded. 'Mrs Boffin.'

'She's given me a note from Robbie.' Beth pushed past her mother and hurried upstairs. She needed to be on her own to read it.

Beth pulled her bedroom door closed and went to the window seat. Hugging her knees to her chest, she thought of Dorothea, an old lady with sad eyes. She used not to have sad eyes – well, not unless she was crying over something Robbie had done. Her eyes used to twinkle with the mischief and daring, she wouldn't actually carry out herself – that was Robbie's role.

But today her sad eyes had to do with Robbie also. He had died. He was gone. Never would Beth see her merry friend again. Never would he poke her, race her, trip her up or do any other mad scheme that entered his jumbled up brain. Beth was sure that now she must have sad eyes too. This was worse than leaving Aisha in London. This was permanent. But, there was something: she crinkled the letter between her fingers. She did have this note. Words from Robbie, the man old enough to be a granddad. A letter written specially for her. Slowly she opened it.

Dear Beth,

If you're reading this, it's because I'm dead. Don't be sad. I've had a better life than I was ever meant to. And it's all thanks to you.

Beth shook her head and re-read the previous sentence. Thanks to her?

You took away my greatest fear: that I was stupid. I was always so angry, with my teachers, with Jack and anyone who could do what I couldn't. But after going to your school and you telling me about dyslexia, I learnt how to see words differently. And when I went back school, I made the teachers understand I wasn't stupid. My father didn't remember anything about our disappearance or all those years he lived alone. He laughed at us for even suggesting it.

But he was different when we got back. He understood me better and valued us more. So I think some part of his subconscious knew what had happened. There was no more talk of sending me to boarding school. If I hadn't met you, I would have gone and burnt down any boarding school that had me. God knows what would have happened to me and anyone else who had got in my way!

But I've three sons now, a daughter and four grandchildren. I married a girl called Linda. She reminds me of you. She's clever and always laughs at my jokes, the way you did, even when you didn't want to.

I'm sorry I was so grumpy with you that last Saturday in Seabury. I was angry because Dad was coming out of hospital and I didn't want my father to be an old man. He died at the ripe old age of ninety-two, and the second time around, we were great friends.

I don't know what happened, when I travelled to your home and you came to mine. I've spent my whole life studying time warps and black holes but found nothing to help me understand it. In the end I decided the house made it happen for some reason, and when Dad died (which I believe he did that day in Seabury) the house called us all home, and that was the end of it. All I know is that I'm glad it happened. You changed my life Beth Boffin and I've never forgotten you.

I hope you're happy now and take no nonsense from girls like Gráinne. She's just insecure and envious, you know, I saw it in her eyes. She reminds me of how I used to be. Some of us don't know how to handle our emotions so we lash out at others. Gráinne's one of them. You're not, though, Beth. You're better than that. A true friend and one of the cleverest people I've ever known. I bet you'll be a teacher, or even a writer. Lucky children who are taught by you.

With love from your friend,

Robbie.

Beth let the note fall. Her vision was blurred. She turned to the window and recalled how the view looked in Robbie's day, when the houses were newly built, old style cars were parked in a few of the drives and women walked up and down the pavement pushing large perambulators with bicycle-sized wheels.

'You changed my life too,' she whispered.

It was true.

Before Robbie tumbled his way into their home, she had been miserable. Her Grandmother was dead, and she'd lost her best friend and home in London. At first it seemed as if Robbie made things a whole lot worse but perhaps good things can sometimes come in disguise: Gráinne, her arch enemy, was now one of her friends at school, Cormac had given up music school and was fun again. Even her mother was different. Inspired by Isabelle, she was growing organic vegetables in the garden and had banned all processed food. And when she was home she really there, not ignoring everyone with her head in a book.

Beth heard the front door click closed and saw Dorothea walk slowly down the drive. At the gate she turned, looked up at the house and waved. Beth lifted her hand in acknowledgement. Dorothea must be lonely now without her brother. Beth hadn't asked what happened to Jack. Maybe he'd emigrated or died young and that's why she hadn't been able to find him.

Well, she would visit Dorothea soon. Her address was written at the top of the letter.

Dorothea Musgrove, 105 Haddington Park, Glenageary, County Dublin.

Yes, she'd visit her and bring back her diary. Beth held the battered old notebook to her chest. They could talk about old times together, and Beth could find out who Mr Musgrove was and how she'd fallen in love with him. It wouldn't feel strange talking to an old woman like Dorothea, because she could remember her so clearly as a shy girl. And when she looked in her eyes she could see the same person again. She'd find out more about Robbie too, and maybe even meet his children and grandchildren. There was a lot he had left behind.

Beth folded the letter, and opened the drawer in her desk. She slipped the letter inside and slid the drawer shut. It was over. But in a way her life in Dublin was only beginning. She was going to secondary school in September. It was to be her second chance to start again. This time she wouldn't have Robbie but she'd remember everything he'd taught her: how to be brave, how to run away when you had to, how to laugh, how not to take things too seriously. And most of all, how to hold out for what you believe in, even when everyone else said you shouldn't. Even your own parents.

'Beth,' her mother called from downstairs.

'Yes?'

'It's dinner time. Are you coming?'

Beth walked over to her bed and ran her hand along the smooth wall. There were no more cracks. Everything was whole again. Number 3 Hawthorn Road was at peace.